SNOW

Sue Brown

BEARYTALES #1

Published by One Hat Press

Cover design by Pippa Wood

Formatting by Format4U/Clare London

A shivering twink, stumbling through the snowy night in a panic. A lonely Daddy bear who needs a boy. Will they find each other before it's too late?

In the Kingdom Mountain theme park, a young kitchen worker dreams of being a boy to a Daddy who loves him, but the evil CEO has other plans for Lyle.

Gruff is built like a bear and with the heart of a Daddy. But as the youngest and smallest of seven gay brothers who live together in the Kingdom Mountain forest, the chances of finding a boy of his own are slim.

Lost in the woods as night falls, Lyle is getting colder by the minute. Will he be saved by the Daddy bear just waiting for a boy like him?

Contents

Chapter 1

LYLE

Exhausted and cold beyond endurance, Lyle longed to lay down and sleep in the snow, but he knew if he did, he'd never wake up. He had to keep going. Somewhere there had to be a shelter; a hut or a cave where he could rest until morning.

He didn't know how long he'd been walking. It felt like hours. He didn't even know how he'd ended up in this forest. Lyle was sure he'd never been here before. He'd never left Kingdom Mountain theme park since the day he was delivered to its door and discovered the hell that lay beyond the wrought iron gates.

He felt as if he were in a fog. He tried to remember, but as soon as he pinpointed one memory, everything became fuzzy. He'd woken up in the dorm and started work in the kitchen as usual, and after that was a blank. He'd suddenly become aware he was stumbling through a forest of pine trees, freezing cold, his mouth dry. And it had only gotten worse, visibility diminishing with each passing step. When had it gotten dark?

As he grew up, he'd stared at the trees beyond the gates, longing to be free to walk in the forests, but to wake up not knowing where he was or what he was doing here…Lyle was more scared than he'd ever been in his eighteen-year-old life.

"Happy eighteenth birthday, Lyle. Today is the day you're going to die."

His voice broke the silence, but it didn't provide any comfort. For so long he'd heard nothing but the harshness of each breath and felt the burning pain of the cold air in his lungs.

He cried out as he sank deeper into the snow and stumbled, falling flat on his face. He wasn't dressed for hiking in snowy terrain. He wore a thin red and yellow jacket that was too big for him, and the battered sneakers that he usually wore for work in the vast kitchens of the theme park. His pants were soaked to the knees from sinking into the snow, and he'd stopped feeling his feet a long while back.

"Please help me, Daddy."

His words, almost fevered, broke the silence again. No one answered him and he sobbed. He didn't have a Daddy, no matter how hard he prayed, and now he was going to die out here unless a miracle happened. But miracles only happened to good boys. And Lyle had spent his whole life being told he was bad.

He swayed, this time falling against a tree, his cheek scraping painfully against the icy bark. When he fell to his knees, he let himself fall all the way until he was face down in the snow. He stayed down, too stunned to move. Maybe he'd just rest here a while and catch his breath.

GRUFF

The fresh snowfall had made traversing the forest harder than usual, and Gruff was ready to go home. Hunting had been poor, and he was thankful for the meat already in the freezer. He couldn't stay too long out here. Darkness was falling, and it was already getting harder to see in the dense forest. If he wasn't careful his brothers would be sending a search party out for him. Despite the fact he knew the forest like the back of his hand, his brothers always worried about him. That was the joy of being the youngest and smallest of seven. Gruff was always going to be the baby. Small was relative term as he was six foot three, with broad shoulders and a massive chest, but PJ was nearly seven feet tall. All the Brenner boys were built on the farside of huge.

Seven boys, all unmarried and still living in the family home, managing the family's Christmas tree farm. They knew the townsfolk talked about them, but by now they ignored it. Folk had learned to be polite to their faces and gossip behind their backs since Damien, the oldest brother, took out Chester Mayfield's teeth when he'd laughed about one of Damien's siblings.

The girls had long since quit trying to throw themselves at any of them. Handsome as they were, the Brenner boys didn't look at girls that way. Everyone knew the Brenner boys were all gay. The women of the town gossiped about how their dear mother must be turning in her grave, and the men opined that their father should have taken a strap to them. The brothers ignored them all. Their wonderful parents had loved them dearly, and the brothers had mourned them hard when a man had liquored up and got behind the wheel of his car. He'd died in the blazing wreck along with their parents.

Gruff was the youngest at twenty-eight, Damien the oldest at forty, and they still lived together. They were all gay, but there was an added complication, which was why they were unattached.

Seven gay Daddies living in a house. That was some complication.

Gruff was happy to be close to home and dreaming of his dinner when something at the base of a tree caught his eye. He squinted, trying to work out what it was. In the middle of the forest, the only colors were the pure-white of the snow and the deep browns and greens of the trees. He didn't expect to see anything red or yellow glinting through the gloom. Heading in the direction of the tree, he was sinking into the snow with every step. Whatever it was, it didn't belong out here, and he didn't want an animal to try to eat it by mistake.

As he got closer, he saw that that it was bigger than he expected, and his heart sank, knowing immediately what it was. They were deep in his family's land. No one would have ventured here by mistake. Gruff braced himself for what he might find. He'd found people in the woods before, frozen to death, miles from help, although never one so close to their home. The forest wasn't a place for the unwary or unprepared. He loved it here, but then he and his brothers had been born on the mountain. They knew what they were doing.

Gruff knelt beside the body, snow already covering the thin red and yellow jacket. Five minutes later and he might not have spotted it. He studied the damp, dark curls and briefest glimpse of pale skin, then rolled the body over gently, and his breath caught.

Gruff sat back on his heels. "Oh, you're barely more than a boy. How did you end up here?"

The dark hair, his face the color of the snow and his lips blue, and an abrasion marring the perfection of his left cheek. The poor boy. How had he gotten trapped up here? The nearest trail was miles away. Usually Gruff left the bodies after snapping a photo and notifying the sheriff's department. But with this pretty one, his heart sank at the idea of leaving him here at the mercy of the predators. Gruff didn't question too closely his motives for taking the little one back with him. He was beyond help now. It just didn't seem right to leave him.

"Why were you here all alone, little snow twink?"

He scooped the body up and put it over his shoulder. Despite the fact the boy could be no taller than five foot eight, he was a dead weight. Gruff wasn't surprised he'd not seen the boy on the way out. The forest was huge, and he'd only spotted him this time by chance. If only he'd found him sooner. How long had the boy been here before succumbing to the cold? Gruff was just thankful in these temperatures, death would have been quick. Small mercies.

It was dark by the time he got home, as it took longer with the additional weight, and he sank to his knees many times. He was relieved when his family's large log cabin eventually came into view. Where would he put the boy to make him safe from the predators? He didn't want to attract stray bears and wolves, and neither did he want a dead body in the home. He could just imagine what his brothers would say about that.

As he approached the cabin, the door burst open and a pile of men, all of them bellowing at the top of their considerable voices, rushed toward him. They were huge and bearded, and all had their father's deep blue eyes.

"Where the hell have you been?" Damien, his eldest brother, snapped.

"We were about to send out a search party," Brad groused.

Gruff tuned out the rest of the complaints. As the youngest of seven brothers he was used to doing that.

"That doesn't look like something we can eat," Jake said, nodding at the body over Gruff's shoulder. He was two years older than Gruff and the next one in line.

"Found him under a tree," Gruff said.

PJ, the middle brother and built like a small tank, folded his arms across his chest. "Why did you bring the body here? It's only going to attract predators."

"He's young," Gruff said. "It didn't seem right

to leave him there alone."

He knelt and laid the body on the ground, gentle even though he knew the boy was beyond caring.

"Jesus," Harry said. He had a shock of bright red hair and when he was being an ass the family called him the prince, because he'd been named after some prince in England who'd been born the same day. "He's a babe."

Gruff looked down at him. "He's a boy."

Not really a boy when he looked closer, a man. A very young man. Gruff's heart ached for what he could have been. The potential, lost with one unwary step off the trail. Was a family hurting somewhere, missing their son? Did they even know he was missing yet? He was glad he wasn't going to have to be the one to deliver that news.

"We'll put him in the barn with the tools. We can lock that until the sheriff can collect him," Alec said. He was number five and always practical.

He went to pick up the body, but Gruff stopped him.

"I'll do it."

He wasn't sure why, but he didn't want anyone else touching him.

As he knelt in the snow, Gruff looked at the boy's face. He blinked and looked closer. He swore he saw a puff of breath coming out of the boy's mouth.

"Hurry up, Gruff. It's freezing out here," Brad complained.

Gruff looked closer. It was difficult to see in the

darkness, but he was sure he saw the boy's lips twitch. "He's alive."

"What?"

The brothers hustled around him. He paid no attention to them, used to their constant jostling. He picked the boy up, feeling the pull in his shoulders at the dead weight. "We need to get him inside now."

His brothers parted like the waves to let him through with his precious bundle. The warmth of the cabin hit him like a blast as he walked in. He hesitated, unsure what to do with the boy.

"Put him on the kitchen table," Harry said.

Gruff grunted in agreement, then headed for the enormous pine kitchen table where they had all their family meals, and laid the boy down gently. His hair looked almost black, as snow and ice melted into little puddles and ran off the table onto the floor.

"We need to get these wet clothes off and get him warmed up," Brad said.

Gruff looked up to see Brad and Harry with him. "Can you get blankets?"

Harry shook his head. "Skin to skin will be best. Take him to your bedroom and get into bed with him."

Gruff stared at him. "What?"

"Body warmth is what he needs," Harry repeated.

"I can't hug a man," Gruff stammered, his cheeks heating up.

"You're gay. You've hugged guys before."

"What if he's not gay? It's not like I can ask him

for consent."

"Then apologize to him when he's not dead," Harry snapped. "For now, he needs to get warm. If you don't want to do it, then one of us can."

"No!" The word erupted out of Gruff's mouth before he thought about it. "I'll do it."

The boy was *his*! No one else could touch him. No one!

He realized he was growling, and he had to take a deep breath to get himself under control.

"Okay then, little brother," Harry said mildly, his tone totally belied by his huge smirk. "Get naked and warm him up."

PJ came in with blankets. Gruff told the three brothers to get out. They saluted him and left. He ignored them all, his attention focused on saving the boy. *His* boy. He carefully peeled off the wet jacket to reveal a sodden, thin, pale green, long-sleeved t-shirt which clung to his skin. He stripped that off too. The boy's smooth chest was almost blue with cold, and he was thin, his ribs showing, as if he never got enough to eat. Gruff covered the top half of him with a blanket and pulled off his sneakers and pants. He hesitated at the briefs, but they were just as wet.

"Get it together," he growled to himself and drew them down the slender legs covered with fine dark hair.

He wrapped the boy up. Not an easy thing to do as the boy was still lax and floppy. Gruff held him close and left the kitchen. Harry had waited for him; the rest of his brothers had disappeared.

Gruff blushed again at Harry's curious

expression, but he said, "Do you think we can save him?"

"I don't know," Harry said. "But now he's got a chance, thanks to you."

Gruff shivered at the thought he might have missed the boy. He'd only been out so late because he'd been tracking hoof prints.

Harry clapped a hand on his shoulder. "You did good, baby brother. I'll come in and check on him when you're settled and bring you something hot to drink. Not for him, mind. He shouldn't be drinking anything hot just yet."

Gruff was touched by Harry's thoughtfulness. In his bedroom, he tugged back the bedclothes and laid his precious burden on the bed. He quickly stripped off down to his boxers, which were dry, then he got into bed, unwrapped the blankets from the boy, and pulled the sheet and comforter over them.

"Skin to skin," he muttered and drew the boy into his arms.

Gruff was huge and the boy half his size. Still, it was like hugging a body-length ice-block. The boy was so cold. Gruff could feel his own body heat leeching away. He should have dried the boy's hair. Rivulets of ice-water ran onto Gruff's chest, making him shiver.

Harry poked his head around the door. "Done? Good. I'll bring you soup."

"And a towel," Gruff said. "I need to dry his hair."

"Be right back."

Gruff relaxed as much as he could. How long

would he have to lie here? As far as he knew, this was a first for the brothers. They'd never found anyone still living before.

Harry returned with a huge mug of home-made vegetable soup and a towel. He handed the towel to Gruff and put the soup on the nightstand.

Gruff tried to dry the boy's hair but it was awkward to hold him and rub his hair at the same time.

"Here, let me," Harry said and reached for the towel.

Gruff couldn't help the growl that seemed to roll up from his chest. He knew intellectually Harry only wanted to help him, but the idea of anyone touching the boy apart from him filled his head with rage.

Harry's eyes went wide, and he stepped back, his hands held up in surrender. "Okay, okay, little brother. He's all yours, I get that. But you can't hold him and dry his hair thoroughly. Let me rub his hair with the towel and dab his cheek with antiseptic, and then I'll leave you alone."

Gruff gave a curt nod, and Harry approached cautiously with the towel. He did exactly as he said. Rubbing the boy's head until it was tousled but at least partially dry and not leaking cold rivers onto Gruff's chest.

Gruff sipped at his soup, appreciating the warmth while Harry did his thing. But finally he wanted to be left alone, so he took the towel out of Harry's hands. "He's fine now. Clean his cheek and leave."

Harry gave him a 'you're being ridiculous' look,

but Gruff didn't care. It was his time to look after the young twink. Harry dabbed at the boy's cheek with an antiseptic wipe, then picked up the wet clothes and left, closing the door behind him. Gruff expelled a sigh of relief, then looked down at the boy. His eyes were still closed, his lashes fanned out on his pale cheeks.

Would he survive? He had to, surely. Gruff wasn't sure who he was praying to as he begged them to keep the boy alive. He would give all his body warmth for the young man. Gruff finished the soup and lay back down on the bed, the boy's head on his chest, body draped over Gruff's. He was thin for sure, but Gruff noticed defined muscle tone, as if he did manual work but never got enough to eat.

Where had the boy come from? Gruff had found bodies on the mountain before. They usually turned out to be walkers who'd lost their way and ended up miles from the trails. But generally, they were at least dressed for hiking. This boy had been wearing a thin jacket and sneakers. The chances of him getting there by mistake was very slim. Had someone tried to kill him? Had he been drugged?

"Who did this to you, my snow twink?"

Gruff's heart ached for the young man and he resolved not to let him out of sight, because he was a Daddy and, somehow, he'd found a boy who needed his help.

Chapter 2

LYLE

Lyle's dreams were vivid and confusing. One minute he was cold to his bones, and the next he was roasting. He dreamed of sleeping under the stars in a snowy wasteland and then being in the softest bed with a drum beating under him. He heard harsh voices, then a growl which promised safety. Hands which hurt him, followed by the gentlest of touches, but nothing made sense. He wondered if he was hallucinating. He feared he was dreaming, and he'd wake up in his hard pallet in the cold, drafty dorm, surrounded by twenty other boys. The drum beat continued, a *thud thud* strangely comforting, and his pillow was kind of hard and tickled his cheek.

He opened his eyes, intending to thump his pillow to try make it softer, only to discover he wasn't sleeping on a pillow. It was a man's chest, muscled and covered in a good amount of hair. Still half-asleep, Lyle was tempted to lie back on the gorgeous chest, stroke the fur, and let the sound of the heartbeat lull him back to sleep.

Chest?

What on earth?

Lyle tried to sit up, only to discover the man's

arms around him, pinning him tight. He looked up to see a handsome bear of a man sleeping peacefully. Lyle studied him for a moment, noting the tousled hair that needed a trim, and a beard that wasn't quite out of control but on the verge of it. Lyle was sure he'd never seen him before. Much as his memory was all fuzzy, he was sure the man was a stranger to him.

Who was he? More to the point, *where were they*?

Lyle looked around the room. He'd never seen a bedroom like this, with dark blue walls and heavy oak furniture. It looked masculine and calm. There were no pictures on the walls, but crimson throws on the chair and armoire broke up the dark colors. Whoever the man was, he was very lucky to sleep in a room like this.

It still didn't explain what Lyle was doing here. Why was Lyle in his bed? Where was his drafty dorm in the theme park? Where were the rest of the boys he'd slept with for over a decade?

Then Lyle looked down and squeaked.

Lyle was laying on top of a naked man.

He was naked.

Panicked, Lyle struggled, trying to free himself, but it was futile. The man had muscles on muscles. Lyle found himself distracted by the curve of those muscles for a moment.

"Focus, Lyle."

He said it out loud. At the sound of his voice, the man's eyelids fluttered open, and Lyle looked into deep blue eyes.

"Wow," he said.

The man looked momentarily confused and then his lips curved into the broadest smile Lyle had ever seen. Lyle was transfixed by the way his smile reached his eyes. He'd never seen men smile like that before.

"You're awake," the man said.

"I am." Lyle wasn't sure what to say.

"That's wonderful."

"Um...who are you and where am I?"

"My name's Gruff Brenner, and you're in my home."

Lyle thought Gruff was a bit of an odd name, but it suited the guy. "I'm Lyle." He couldn't remember his second name. No one had ever used it. "I'm in your bed."

"Yes."

"Naked."

Gruff nodded. "Harry thought it would be the best thing."

"He did? Who's Harry?" Lyle shook his head, trying to focus on his main concern. "Why am I stark naked in your bed?"

"Harry's my brother. I found you in the forest. You were ice-cold and in soaking wet clothes. Harry suggested skin-to-skin contact would warm you up better than blankets."

Lyle suddenly remembered the vivid dreams of being frozen cold and falling asleep in the snow. So, they hadn't been dreams. But how did he end up in the forest?

Meanwhile Gruff was still talking. "Nothing inappropriate happened."

"Thank you." Lyle held back a laugh, aware he

was on the verge of a full-blown panic attack. He was naked and hugging a strange man in his bed, and nothing inappropriate happened? "I'm warm now."

"That's good," Gruff said enthusiastically, but although his embrace loosened a fraction, he still didn't let go. "How did you end up in the forest?"

Lyle furrowed his brow. "I don't remember. It's all a blank. I woke up and I was cold and wet and walking in the snow. I don't know how I got there."

"How did you get the cut on your cheek?" Gruff brushed it gently and Lyle flinched. "Sorry."

"It's okay." Gruff's touch had been soft, not meaning to cause him pain. Lyle tried to remember how he'd hurt his cheek. "I'm not sure. I remember stumbling against a tree. Maybe then?"

"Where do you live?"

"I…I don't know." Lyle stared at Gruff and the panic took more of a hold. "I think I sleep in a dorm room with other boys, but I don't know where."

Gruff made a rumbling noise and held Lyle close. "It's okay, Lyle, it's okay. We'll find out. Jake's good at that sort of thing. You're safe here."

Lyle found himself smushed against Gruff's furry chest. It was like hugging a huge bear, and Lyle didn't want to move. Gruff represented safety, and right now he was the only thing anchoring Lyle.

"Who's Jake?" Lyle asked.

"My brother."

"You have two brothers?"

Gruff's chest leaped under him as he laughed. "I have six brothers."

"Wow."

"I know. We all live here."

Lyle raised his head. "In the same house?"

Gruff shrugged. "Yeah, we get along most of the time, and it's a really big house. We call it the cabin, but it's huge."

"I don't think I have any brothers or sisters."

"I'm sorry."

Lyle shrugged. At the moment it was the least of his concerns. "It's okay. I wish I could remember where I lived though."

"We'll work it out. You know your name and the fact you sleep in a dorm room. That's a start." Gruff said. "You remember dreams?"

But before Lyle could answer, the door opened and a man walked in, holding clothes Lyle recognized as his. He had flaming red hair, and a huge bushy beard which was the same vibrant color as his hair. But Lyle could tell he was one of Gruff's brothers from the curve of his mouth and the deep blue eyes, the same as Gruff's. This must be Harry.

"Hey, he's awake."

From Harry's intense stare, Lyle felt as if he was some sort of circus animal, and Harry was just waiting for him to perform.

"We've just woken up," Gruff said. "What time is it?"

"After eight. I was just checking how our guest was and if you needed a replacement warm body.

I came in earlier, but you were both asleep."

Under Lyle, Gruff stiffened, and he heard what he was sure was a growl. "Lyle's mi…fine."

Did Gruff nearly say 'mine'? Lyle stared at him. That sounded almost possessive.

But Harry just laughed. "Okay. Well, if you don't want the whole family coming in and seeing you cuddling, you'd better get up and come downstairs. Lyle, is it? I washed and dried your clothes, but I'm afraid the sneakers and jacket are beyond saving."

"Th…thanks," Lyle stammered, touched that Harry would have gone to that trouble for him.

Harry waited.

"You can go now," Gruff growled. "You don't get to see him naked."

Harry heaved out a sigh and chuckled before leaving the room.

Gruff huffed out a breath. "I'm sorry, he's an ass, but you'd better know before you walk into the lions' den, they're all asses, and as the baby of the family I'm usually their target. Just give as good as you get."

Lyle wasn't sure whether to feel worried for himself or sorry for Gruff. "I'll try."

And finally, Gruff let go of Lyle, almost reluctantly it seemed.

Lyle sat up. "I need the bathroom."

Gruff pointed to a door. "Through there. Do you want a shower too?"

A shower. For real? He wasn't sure it was his day to take a shower.

"I can have a shower?" At Gruff's sudden frown

he became aware he'd said something wrong. "I don't have to. I'll be fine without one, honestly."

"Of course, you can have a shower, Lyle. Come with me, and I'll show you how it works." Gruff slid out of bed.

Lyle stood too, but the sudden rush to his head was too much and he swayed. Gruff was there in an instant, holding him steady.

"Sorry," Lyle murmured, conscious of the strong hard body he leaned again.

"No need to apologize," Gruff assured him. "Do you feel okay to walk now?"

Lyle nodded, and Gruff guided him to the bathroom, his hand on Lyle's lower back. It was comforting and a little overwhelming. He couldn't remember the last time someone took care of him like this. Mind you, as he couldn't remember anything except his name and where he slept, that probably didn't mean much.

The bathroom was small, dominated by the huge shower stall.

Gruff caught Lyle's wide-eyed stare. "I'm a big man. I need space. You should see Damien's bathroom. You could hold a party in there."

"This'll do fine." Lyle felt almost giddy at the prospect.

Gruff showed him how to turn it on and then turned to leave him.

In a sudden panic, Lyle clutched at his arm. "Don't leave me alone."

"I'll just be in the bedroom," Gruff assured him, patting his hand. His large hand covered Lyle's.

"You promise?"

"I promise."

Lyle breathed easier. He wanted to ask Gruff to stay in the bathroom, but he knew that would be odd, so he let Gruff go.

He did his business and then turned on the shower, still marveling at the fact Gruff would let him take a shower without checking what day it was. The feel of the hot water was indescribably wonderful. He closed his eyes and let it run over his face, ignoring the sting of his cheek. Lyle knew one more thing about himself. Wherever he lived he didn't have showers like this, and he wasn't allowed to just have a shower whenever he wanted.

Gruff seemed to have an entire store of shower gels, shampoos and conditioners, all with names Lyle didn't recognize. He sniffed at one. It had a woodsy scent. He put that back hastily. He'd had more than enough to do with trees. He picked up a green curved bottle. It was a floral scent but light. That was okay. He'd use that. He turned to look at the bottle and saw the castle logo.

Evil! Instantly he felt as if he were being swallowed up by a huge wave of malevolence and he screamed.

GRUFF

Gruff knew he'd told Lyle to take as long as he liked, but it had been fifteen minutes and he hadn't heard anything from the bathroom.

He hesitated, not wanting to disturb the boy if he was enjoying the shower. Especially as it sounded like he'd never been allowed a shower like that before. He paced around the bed, worrying at the lack of noise, until he told himself to channel his inner Daddy. He knocked, then went into the bathroom without waiting for a response.

At first he couldn't see Lyle, as the bathroom was full of steam. He flapped his hand in front of him and it cleared the steam long enough to spy Lyle curled up in a fetal position on the floor of the shower stall. Gruff rushed forward and opened the door, slamming off the water before he got soaking wet. He knelt and touched Lyle's shoulder. The boy flinched away.

"Lyle, what's wrong? What happened?"

Lyle didn't move, didn't say a word. Gruff was unsure what to do, but he couldn't leave him soaking wet and cold after taking all that time to warm him up. Gruff grabbed a towel and wrapped Lyle in it. Then he scooped him up and carried him back to the bed. As they sat together, Lyle wrapped his arms around Gruff's neck and hung on for dear life, shaking violently.

Gruff held him close, rumbling soothing nothings in his ear. Anything to calm him down. "It's all right, my boy, I've got you. Your Daddy's got you. It's okay, my boy. Daddy's here." He didn't focus on what he was saying, just repeating the words over and over until Lyle subsided in his arms, worn out. Gruff stroked his hair, feeling it damp under his fingertips again.

Lyle let out a sigh which seemed to be drawn up from his toes, and buried his head in Gruff's neck. "I'm sorry."

"Nothing to be sorry for, boy."

Gruff held him tightly, wanting Lyle to draw strength from him. He had no idea what had set him off in the shower, but he needed to find out before they stepped downstairs.

He heard footsteps in the hallway and his door opened. Harry stood there, a huge smirk on his face when he saw Gruff holding Lyle, but the amusement slipped away when Gruff shook his head.

"What's wrong?" Harry mouthed.

"I don't know," Gruff mouthed back.

He was eternally grateful Harry picked up on his vibe and vanished, leaving Gruff alone with his distraught boy.

As the door shut, Lyle raised his head. He looked calm but exhausted, deep shadows under his eyes. "Thank you."

"What for?"

"Coming when I screamed."

Gruff frowned and shook his head. "You didn't scream, Lyle. You didn't make a sound."

Lyle sat up straighter, his brow furrowed. "But I was screaming out loud."

"Baby, you didn't make a sound. I came in to check on you and you were curled up in the shower."

"I...heard screams. I'm sure I was screaming." He furrowed his brows. "Was it another dream? It seemed so real."

"Your dreams have been real so far, boy." Gruff said. "Do you know what happened? What made you scream?"

Lyle's face grew pinched and he dropped his gaze, refusing to meet Gruff's eyes. "No."

The boy couldn't lie to save his life.

"Boy." Gruff projected a stern voice and Lyle shivered. "Don't lie to me. You're a rotten liar, and I won't have it. Now tell me what happened."

"It's stupid," Lyle whispered, still refusing to look at Gruff.

"Just tell me."

Lyle ran his hand through his damp hair, sending strands everywhere. Gruff wanted to smooth it down. "I picked up one of the bottles in your shower. This is so stupid. It had a castle on it."

Gruff thought for a moment. "The green one? From Kingdom Mountain?"

The instant shudder that went through Lyle was answer enough. Gruff didn't need to hear the barely audible whisper to know that whatever flashback the bottle evoked was not the happy ever after kind.

"What did you remember?"

"It wasn't so much a memory but like something evil was going to attack me. That's all I can remember. Just this overwhelming feeling of evil. I screamed. I screamed." He slumped. "At least I thought I screamed."

Gruff held the boy close to him, feeling helpless to help his boy. Whatever had happened to Lyle was traumatic enough to evoke a powerful reaction. Gruff wasn't sure if he wanted Lyle's memories to return or not. Was he better off not knowing what had happened to him?

He heard Lyle's stomach rumble and realized the boy hadn't eaten since he woke up. "Let's go downstairs and get something to eat."

Lyle nodded listlessly, but he didn't make a move. Gruff stood and plopped Lyle on the bed. Then he took the clothes Harry had washed and dried, and dressed Lyle as if he were a small child.

He picked Lyle up into his arms, saying, "We're going downstairs to get food and drink."

He expected Lyle to refuse, but instead he buried his head in the crook of Gruff's neck and sighed.

"Okay."

Yes, Daddy. Gruff longed to correct him but he hadn't the right, and that was a whole other conversation.

Gruff took the stairs carefully, carrying Lyle as if he was precious cargo. He paused, hearing voices, but he knew he couldn't avoid his brothers forever. When he walked into the kitchen, the conversation died instantly, and six pairs of eyes snapped to look at him.

"Lyle," he rumbled, "meet my brothers."

Lyle raised his head and for the first time, Gruff saw a genuine smile on his face. "Hi." He received a chorus of "Howdy," and "Hi," in return.

Gruff put Lyle down. He felt nerves get the better of the boy, and Lyle clung onto him, but Gruff put an arm around Lyle's shoulders and guided him to Gruff's usual seat at the table between Jake and Brad, then he pointed at Damien at the other end of the table.

"Lyle, that's Damien, he's the oldest and the

only one beside me that you have to listen to." He ignored the hoots and catcalls. "The rest of them can introduce themselves while I make us a drink. Do you like hot chocolate?"

Lyle's eyes went wide for a moment, with the same shocked surprise as when Gruff had mentioned the shower. "Yes please."

"Marshmallows too?"

Lyle nodded mutely as if he was overcome.

Gruff avoided the curious gazes of his brothers as he went to the stove. When they started introducing themselves, and with his back to the table, Gruff allowed himself to react. He clenched his jaw so tight it hurt. His poor boy. Wherever Lyle lived there had been few luxuries if a shower and a simple cup of hot chocolate provoked such a reaction.

As he expected, there was a large pan of hot chocolate ready to pour. He tipped the thick chocolate into two mugs and topped them with fluffy marshmallows.

"Where's ours?" Damien said as he returned to the table.

"Get your own," Gruff returned.

He handed one mug to Lyle who stared at it as if he wasn't sure what to do with it.

"This is for me?" Lyle asked.

Gruff nodded. He stood behind Lyle, his hand on his shoulder to provide comfort and, he had to admit to himself, giving his brothers an unsubtle hands-off warning. Lyle was his and he wasn't going to share.

Men came and went at the house. They weren't

celibate by any means, it was just no one seemed to stay. Gruff had had his share of boyfriends, but it seemed they were all looking for something other than Gruff. He had been prepared to wait for the right boy, although he'd never expected to find him half-frozen in the snow. Would Lyle feel the same about him?

His brothers were involved in an intense discussion about something they'd watched on TV earlier. Gruff felt his frayed nerves unwinding as he listened to their usual bickering. The hot chocolate was soothing, and from the happy noises Lyle made as he sipped the drink, he was in heaven. Lyle looked up at him and Gruff grinned down at his chocolate mustache. He wiped Lyle's top lip with his thumb and sucked on it. Lyle's eyes went wide as he tracked the gesture.

"Get a room," PJ muttered.

Lyle flushed, and Gruff growled. To his surprise, PJ subsided without a word.

But the easy relaxed atmosphere couldn't last, and it was shattered abruptly when Damien said, "So Lyle, how come you ended up in our forest?"

Lyle went tense under Gruff's hands.

"It's okay, Lyle, you don't have to answer if you don't want to," Gruff said, scowling at his brother. Damien ignored him, his whole attention focused on Lyle.

Lyle put his mug down on the table, his eyes wide and worried. "It's not that I don't want to answer you. It's that I don't know how I ended up there. I remember going to work, and I woke up in your forest, and everything in between is a blank."

Chapter 3

LYLE

"You don't remember anything?" The oldest brother raised an eyebrow. He looked skeptical, and Lyle couldn't blame him. It probably wasn't every day they found a man half-frozen on their doorstep.

"I have flashbacks," he admitted, "but I'm not sure if they're memories or dreams."

"Of what?" one of the younger brothers asked. Lyle couldn't remember what he was called.

"Going to work in the kitchen. Being shouted at, then walking through the snow and not knowing where I was. People hurt me." He wrapped his arms around himself. "I think men hurt me all the time, but I don't know why. I can't remember. What did I do to make them hurt me? I don't even know if it's real." He looked up to see the horrified expressions on the brothers' faces and wanted to run away. In seconds, Gruff lifted him up and sat him on his lap, wrapping his strong arms around him.

"It's all right. You're safe with us. No one hurt you here, I promise."

Lyle was starting to crave the feeling of Gruff holding him, keeping him safe. It stopped him feeling the need to run away. Nothing bad could happen while Gruff held him.

"Enough questions," Gruff said firmly. "Lyle is staying here until his memory returns."

Lyle looked at him. "I can't—"

"Yes, you can."

"I can cook and clean," Lyle said. "I think I'm used to cooking for a large number of people. I can remember working in a kitchen."

"Done," Damien said. "We've got a busy few days ahead with the Christmas harvest. Lyle here can take care of the house while we cut down the trees."

Confused, Lyle turned to Gruff who explained, "We grow Christmas trees. It's time to chop them down and deliver them to town. This time of year, we all help with cutting down the trees and delivering them. By the time we get in we're usually exhausted. It will be good to come home to a cooked meal. And talking of cooked meals—"

Lyle jumped off his lap. "I can start now."

Gruff frowned, but the really big brother beamed at him. "Great. There isn't too much to do tonight. Meat is in the oven. And the baked potatoes are ready."

Ignoring how tired he felt, Lyle hurried over to the stove. If he proved he could take care of the household maybe they'd let him stay. He saw the big slab of beef and his mouth watered. Would they let him have the scraps afterward? He was so hungry, and he couldn't remember the last time he ate.

In thirty minutes, Lyle put a plate heaped with

meat and potatoes and peas in front of each brother. They didn't seem to have much in the way of vegetables, but he'd made a green salad too and fussed until they took a portion. Gruff's face had gotten darker as he cooked, and he couldn't work out what was wrong. He slunk away to clean the pans as the brothers started to eat.

"Lyle!" Gruff barked.

Lyle jumped and nearly dropped the roasting pan. He hurried back to Gruff. "Yes, sir."

They all stopped eating to stare at him, and Gruff eyed him as if he'd grown another head.

"You don't have to call me sir," Gruff said.

"Sorry, sir, I mean, Gruff," Lyle stammered, unsure why Gruff was so angry.

"Where's your dinner?"

"I'm not allowed to eat until everybody's finished. I can make myself a bowl of oatmeal when you're done."

Again, he was aware of the conversation dying and all the brothers turning to stare at him. What did he say wrong this time?

"Fix yourself a plate of food and eat with us," Gruff ordered.

"I—"

"Just sit," PJ said, "before my brother has a conniption."

Lyle wasn't sure what a conniption was, but it didn't sound good. And Gruff's gaze was so steely, Lyle rushed back to the stove and put the smallest amount of meat on a little plate and came back to add green salad.

Gruff took the plate out of his hands and went

back to the beef. Lyle held back a whimper. Wasn't he even allowed a small slice? Then he told himself not to be greedy. Salad would be fine. Gruff returned, and Lyle blinked at the larger plate piled high with meat and a baked potato with peas.

"Sit next to me," Gruff said. "Budge up, Jake."

Jake obligingly moved up and Gruff placed Lyle's plate on the table and pointed to the chair. Lyle sat and stared at the food.

Gruff handed him a knife and fork. "Eat."

Lyle stared at him and then back to the plate. He'd never been allowed food like this before; he was sure of it.

"Lyle, please eat," Gruff insisted.

The beef melted on Lyle's tongue. He had to hold back a moan. And the potato was fluffy and dripping with butter. He ate as much as he could before his stomach was full. But when he looked at his plate, he'd barely eaten anything.

"Lyle," Gruff growled at him.

Lyle hung his head, mortified to have disappointed Gruff. "I'm sorry, but I'm full up."

Indeed, the beef was churning horribly in his stomach. He breathed deeply and after a while the nausea settled. He realized Gruff had put an arm around his shoulder to hold him. Lyle leaned in close, glad of the comfort.

Gruff looked at his brothers. "I'm taking Lyle up to the small bedroom. He can start work tomorrow. You can clear up."

Lyle wanted to protest that he was fine to wash up and clear everything away, but he was suddenly exhausted and needed to sleep.

"We get up at five and eat a cooked breakfast at eight," Damien said. "Lyle, we'll leave you a list of chores on the table."

Lyle flinched at his loud tone, and Gruff asked him what the matter was in a low voice. He shook his head. "I should clear up." He didn't want to let Gruff down just because he was tired.

"Not tonight. You're going to bed now."

Gruff picked him up and Lyle wrapped his arms around Gruff's neck. He was too tired to argue. He would get up early and clean and make breakfast. He closed his eyes and fell asleep to the gentle rhythm of Gruff's stride.

Lyle awoke with a start, disoriented, the sound of loud chatter and the front door banging driving away the last vestiges of sleep. Where was he? He frantically sorted through his memories until he remembered. Gruff, huge bear, his home. He looked around the small bedroom. Unlike Gruff's, it looked impersonal, as if no one slept in here. Then he spied a small bear on one of shelves. Maybe it had been one of the brothers' rooms when they were small.

He couldn't help wondering why he hadn't slept with Gruff, and then told himself to get over it. Just because Gruff had taken care of him didn't mean to say he wanted Lyle there twenty-four/seven, sharing his bed.

Then Lyle remembered what he was supposed to be doing.

Oh no, he was late!

He'd intended to get up at three, his usual time to start preparing the meals for the day but no one had set an alarm and he'd slept through. He looked at the clock on the nightstand. Just after five. They must be so angry with him.

He jumped out of the small bed and looked down at himself. Gruff must have undressed him. He skinned into his pants and long-sleeved T-shirt and ran down the stairs. There was a piece of paper on the table. He ignored that and got busy making breakfast.

GRUFF

"I'm so hungry," Jake said as he climbed the stoop, and there was a general rumble of agreement.

Gruff felt the pull of his muscles and he rolled his shoulders. They'd worked solidly for three hours chopping down the trees ready for this year. He called out for Lyle as soon as they walked in the house, but there was only silence.

"Where's the boy?" Damien bellowed. "He hasn't done the grates. That was first on the list."

Gruff thought Damien's irritation had a lot to do with the fact he hated the job and had been more than happy to pass it onto someone else, but he was surprised that Lyle had ignored the list. He'd seemed so anxious to help.

"You'd better find him," Brad muttered, "before Damien has an aneurysm. He's just the right age."

He chuckled as Damien cursed at him.

Gruff was more concerned about where Lyle

had disappeared to. He searched through the house, worry knotting his gut when they didn't find him in his bedroom.

He pointed out that in each room their beds were made with fresh linen and the bathrooms were cleaner than he'd ever seen them.

"He's the best cleaner we've had," Brad said. "We'll keep him, when we find him."

"He still didn't sweep the grates," Damien grumbled.

Finally they entered the kitchen, and found the table laid for breakfast just as they'd ordered with hot oatmeal on the stove. And stacks of pancakes, waffles, bacon, and eggs.

Damien snorted at the brothers' cries of joy. "Don't get used to it."

Gruff glowered at him. The breakfast had been more than expected, the cleaning was perfect. Damien could clean the damn grate himself. Lyle must have worked himself to the bone to get all this ready. But where was he?

All the brothers sat down and helped themselves to food. Gruff couldn't eat. Worry coiled in his stomach. Had something happened to him?

Then Harry snorted. "Found your boy." He pointed over to the far corner of the kitchen, near the mud room.

Gruff squinted and spied Lyle. What was he doing curled up on the floor? He pushed back his chair, had to grab the back to stop it falling over, then rushed over to Lyle. He knelt beside him but, to his relief, Lyle was just fast asleep.

"He's sleeping," he said.

"Wake him up then?" Damien barked. "He's got the grates to clean, the chickens to feed, and the horses to muck up."

"Then he can chop wood," Brad added.

Gruff's hands curved into fists. "No."

"What?"

"I said no."

He turned to see them all staring at him in shock. Two of them had spoons halfway to their mouths, the oatmeal dripping into their bowls.

"He is not your servant, not your houseboy, or garden boy, or anything else, and certainly not your stable boy. Those are your jobs, not his. You want a full-time cook and cleaner, find your own boy. Lyle is mine."

"But we've got the trees—"

Gruff cut Damien off. "We have to harvest the trees every year. Get over it."

He turned his back on his brothers and gently shook Lyle's shoulder. "Lyle, wake up."

Lyle blinked, opening his eyes slowly to reveal those beautiful brown eyes. "Hey, Dad...Gruff. Sorry, I just needed a nap. Is everything okay? Is the laundry finished? I just need to iron the sheets. Then I'll clean the grates."

Gruff ignored Damien's crow behind him. His breath caught in his throat. Did Lyle almost call him Daddy? He didn't dare hope. "You can rest now. You've done enough."

Gruff scooped Lyle as if he weighed nothing and held him close. He turned back to his brothers. "Do you have something to say to Lyle for all the work he's done?"

"Uh, yeah, thanks Lyle. The bathrooms looked amazing," Brad said.

"And it's the best breakfast ever," PJ piped up. "Thank you."

Lyle looked at Gruff. "What do you want me to do next?"

"Nothing. You're going to sleep."

"But—"

"No buts," Gruff said firmly. "You need to sleep."

Lyle sighed and buried his face into Gruff's shoulder. He yawned and settle down like he belonged in Gruff's arms.

Gruff stalked out of the kitchen and up the stairs. At the top he paused. He desperately wanted to put Lyle into his bed, but he didn't want to make Lyle think that was part of his duties too. So he went to the end of the hallway into Lyle's room and gently placed him on the bed.

Lyle looked worried. "Are you going to throw me out because I can't keep up with the work? I didn't mean to let you down. Please let me try again."

Gruff growled a little, and Lyle shrank back. Angry at himself for scaring the beautiful boy, Gruff knelt in front of him and held out his hand. Tentatively, Lyle put his hand in Gruff's much larger one. Gruff closed his fingers around Lyle's and looked into his eyes.

"You don't have to do any more chores, Lyle. It was wrong of us to make you. You are our guest."

Lyle looked horrified. "I can't be that."

"Why not?"

"I'm a kitchen boy, not a guest."

"You're my guest, Lyle, not the kitchen boy." Gruff squeezed his hand. "And now you need to catch up on your sleep." He tugged Lyle to his feet, pulled back the comforter and pushed him under. "Lie down, and I'll cover you up."

"I'm not used to sleeping in a bed," Lyle confessed. "It's been a long time since I had a bed of my own."

He sounded overwhelmed, and Gruff's heart broke just a little more for him. "Go to sleep, little one. I'll stay here with you until you do. When you wake you find me, okay?"

"Okay." Lyle held out his hand, and Gruff took it. "Thank you, Gruff."

"You're welcome, boy."

Lyle's eyes widened. He gave the smallest of smiles, closed his eyes and was asleep in seconds. Gruff stayed where he was for a long while, Lyle's hand in his, not wanting to move. Lyle was going to be his boy, Gruff was sure of it, but he wouldn't push him. Lyle needed to be treated like a precious gem.

Hunger drove him back down to the kitchen, although he knew there would be little food left with all his brothers there. They were still all round the table and, as the conversation stopped when he walked in the room, it wasn't hard to guess what they'd been talking about.

"You can keep talking about me," he said dryly.

He was surprised to see his plate and mug still

on the table with his usual breakfast foods.

"Oatmeal in the pan," Harry muttered. "You'll have to heat it up. We saved you waffles and bacon. PJ ate all the pancakes."

"Thanks," Gruff said, choked up, because if he missed breakfast most days it would be gone by the time he got to the table.

"Where's Lyle?" Brad asked.

Gruff looked over his shoulder as he stirred the remainder of the oatmeal in the pan. "In his bed."

"Not your bed?" Damien asked slyly.

"Not yet. We haven't discussed anything." He glared at his brothers. "I don't want you stirring the pot until I've had a chance to talk to him."

He would have laughed at the faux expressions of outrage on his brothers' faces if he hadn't been serious. He turned back to the oatmeal, waited until it was steaming nicely, and ladled it into his bowl. Then he sat down at his usual place.

"Your boy makes good oatmeal," Harry said and there was a nod of agreement around the table. "Better than we do. Perhaps he could show us how to make it."

"If he wants to," Gruff said before he took a mouthful.

"Damn, little bro's really possessive about his house-boy," PJ jeered.

Gruff knew PJ was just trying to wind him up, but he had to hold back before he planted one in PJ's smug mouth.

"Lay off, PJ. Gruff really likes Lyle, and this is the first time our little brother's fallen in love." Damien leered at him.

Gruff choked, the oatmeal spraying everywhere.

Brad leapt from his chair. "Jeez, Gruff, that's disgusting!"

It took Gruff time to quit coughing and get his breathing under control. He flailed out a hand, and someone gave him a glass of water.

"I'm not in love," he finally managed.

Brad huffed. "We waited all that time for you to lie to our faces?"

"I'm not lying. I don't…I can't…it's one day, it's too soon."

Harry shook his head. "Then give him to me."

Gruff snarled at him. Harry raised his eyebrows, and Gruff slumped back in his chair. "Shit."

Brad patted him reassuringly on the shoulder. "Don't worry, little bro, it happens to us all." He paused for dramatic effect. "So they tell me."

"I just want to be his Daddy."

"Then be his Daddy," PJ said. "He ain't gonna say no."

Gruff looked around the table. "You're all so calm about it."

Harry stuck a meaty arm around Gruff's neck and dragged him in close. "Nah, we're jealous as all get out, but we love our little brother and want him to be happy. Now hurry up and eat. As your little boy is now off the market, we've got work to do. We need to get the top trees chopped down before the snow gets too deep."

His brothers scattered in various directions, yelling at each other. Gruff topped his mug off with coffee and sat back down at the table. He needed to think for a moment. In love with Lyle? Could it really be that quick?

He shook his head. No, he couldn't be in love, but he was definitely possessive. He'd proved that already. Lyle was his, and no one was going to touch him without Lyle's consent and his permission.

He cleared away his bowl, cup and pan, placing the last of the oatmeal in a small bowl for Lyle if he wanted it. Then he headed upstairs and found a pen and notepad in his own room. Gruff tip-toed into Lyle's room. The boy was still asleep. He placed the note on the nightstand and quietly left the room.

Chapter 4

LYLE

Lyle woke up, completely disoriented and too warm. The bed was much softer than the pallet he was used to sleeping on and he felt smothered by the covers. He opened his eyes and stared up at an unfamiliar ceiling.

"Where am I?"

Then he remembered he was in a guest room in Gruff's home.

He looked down and discovered he was fully dressed in his T-shirt and pants. Then he remembered Gruff putting him to bed. Lyle felt his cheeks flame. Had Gruff really carried him to bed again?

What about his chores? The brothers must be furious with him. It was only his first day and he'd failed. He leaped out of bed, stretching his muscles and rolling his shoulders.

There was a piece of paper on the nightstand. He ignored it and rushed out of the room.

The kitchen was empty. No sign of any of the men, but the table and countertops were clear. Someone had taken time to clean away breakfast.

He wasn't sure what to do next. He looked at the clock. Ten after eleven. Maybe they needed lunch. He looked in the refrigerator. He saw a bowl of oatmeal covered in saran wrap. His stomach growled but he ignored it. It wasn't time for his one meal of the day.

The brothers would need food for lunch. He decided on sandwiches and chips which would give him more time to make something for their dinner. Lyle whistled as he sliced the bread and piled meat and cheese into different sandwiches.

He heard the front door open and stood quickly, swaying as he felt a little dizzy. The table was laden with plenty of food for the men. He hoped they would be happy with him. Lyle smiled as Damien walked into the kitchen, followed by Brad, PJ, Harry. His smile slipped a little when Gruff didn't appear.

Damien stopped short when he saw the table. "What the...did you do this for us?"

Harry pushed past with a wide smile and hungry eyes. "Who else would he be doing this for, dipshit? Does Gruff know?" He sounded a bit worried by that.

"Good food," Brad said, and PJ grunted in agreement.

"Wash your hands," Lyle insisted.

They stared at him, but he must have looked fierce because they all went to the sink and washed up before sitting down. Lyle winced at the dirt marks left on the towel, but he didn't insist they wash their hands again. He wasn't going to push his luck.

"Where's Gruff?" Lyle asked.

"He's talking to Alec and Jake. Don't worry.

He'll be here soon," Damien said in an oddly soothing tone.

"If he isn't, all the food will be gone," Harry chortled.

"He'll kill you if you don't leave any food," Brad said. Then he noticed Lyle's wide-eyed expression. "Don't worry, Gruff will make it painless. But he likes his food. Never get between him and his dinner."

"If his boy is making dinner, he'll be golden," PJ pointed out.

There was a lot to unpack there. Not least of which was the careless 'boy '. Since when had he been Gruff's boy?

Lyle ignored the whispered 'since the first moment you saw him' in his mind.

Then the front door opened again, there was a blast of cold air, and an equally loud blast of chatter, and the three remaining brothers walked through, all talking at the top of their voices.

"Oh good, more food!" Alec said, and headed straight for the table. Jake followed him, reaching for the food before Lyle said in the loudest voice he could manage, "Wash your hands first."

"You've got to do it, dude," Damian said. "He won't let you eat otherwise."

To Lyle's astonishment, the two brothers went and washed their hands, grumbling all the while. But Gruff stood where he was, frowning between his eyes. Lyle looked at him worriedly, concerned he'd done something wrong, and the feeling only intensified when Gruff took him by the elbow and walked him out of the kitchen.

Gruff looked down at Lyle. "Did you make lunch?"

"Yes, I did. I thought you'd be hungry. Did I do something wrong?" Lyle asked shakily.

"I thought I'd made it clear you're not our servant, you are our guest. And you don't have to do take care of us. We should be taking care of you. Didn't you read my note?"

"What note?" Lyle said, all the while his mind frantically racing. How was he going to get out of this one?

"I put it on the nightstand," Gruff said.

"I must have missed it," Lyle said airily. "It must have fallen off."

He knew he had said the right thing when Gruff relaxed.

"Okay, well, I just want you to know that you don't have to take care of us. Otherwise my brothers will have you doing the cooking until eternity. We all hate cooking," Gruff confessed.

Lyle chuckled. "I love cooking," he admitted, "and I am willing to do it as long as I don't have to do the clearing up."

"We'll talk about it later. First let's eat before they finish all the sandwiches."

"Make sure you wash your hands first," Lyle instructed.

Gruff pulled a face but he did as he was told, going to the sink and pushing up his sleeves over the thick forearms. Lyle's mouth watered at the sight.

When Gruff had seated himself, Lyle served him with a sandwich and a heap of chips.

Gruff frowned. "Sit down. You need to eat too."

"Oh, my oatmeal is in the fridge. I'll eat later."

"You'll eat now," Gruff said flatly.

Conversation died around the table, and they all turned to look at Lyle. He felt his cheeks flame.

"I am not supposed to eat with you," he whispered.

"Who said?" PJ asked.

"It is the rules," Lyle explained. "The CEO allowed us one meal a day, but it had to be after everybody else had eaten."

They all stared at him like he'd grown another head. Lyle was tempted to touch the side of his neck just confirm there wasn't a new head growing.

Gruff looked confused. "Who's the CEO?"

Lyle stared at him, then looked away. "I don't know. I just remember his rules."

Gruff didn't look convinced but he nodded. "When did you last eat?"

Lyle didn't answer.

Gruff put down his sandwich and turned to face Lyle. He held out his hand and, hesitantly, Lyle put his much smaller hand in Gruff's. Gruff tugged him closer.

"When I ask a question, I expect you to answer it. When did you last eat?"

"Last night," Lyle whispered, flinching as at least two of the brothers hissed.

Gruff sighed heavily and held Lyle close against him. "While you live with us, you will eat three meals a day and any snacks you want. I don't care what this CEO said. You're not with him anymore. You're with us and we eat a lot."

All the brothers nodded in agreement.

"No point starving yourself, little dude," Brad said.

The next thing Lyle knew, he had a cheese sandwich in one hand and a handful of chips in the other, and he was being told to eat, as Damien told a raucous story about Gruff as a small child.

Gruff was groaning, and his cheeks were crimson as he begged Damien to stop, but that just spurred all the brothers to spill their little brother stories. Lyle couldn't remember the last time his belly ached from laughing so much. He was also acutely conscious that he was now sitting on Gruff's lap again, but no one seemed to care. Gruff seemed unable not to hold him when they were all at the table.

Lyle couldn't believe how fast the food disappeared. He barely ate more than half a sandwich, and when Gruff protested, he pointed out that he'd lived on oatmeal for years, and half a sandwich was more than he'd had for a long time. He remembered making the huge pans of oatmeal and serving them up. There had been very little left for the kitchen workers. This led to a few angry growls around the table, and he flinched, but Gruff held him close and told him that the brothers weren't angry at him but the situation he'd been in.

"I don't know who this CEO is, but he sounds like a crock of shit, making you work long days with no food," Alec said.

"If you remember who he is, we could put a

stop to it," Harry suggested.

Lyle shook his head. "I can't remember."

Gruff held him close and whispered, "It's all right, my boy. You'll remember, but in the meantime, you're safe here."

"I know," Lyle murmured.

But for how long, when they discovered who the CEO truly was? Oh yes, he'd remembered, but how long was he going to be able to hide it?

GRUFF

Gruff was much troubled by Lyle's comments at lunch, and he resolved to talk to his brothers about it later in the day, out of Lyle's hearing. He could see by the frowns on his brothers' faces and the worried expressions they kept shooting at Lyle that they were bothered too. Everything Lyle said about this mysterious CEO and the way he treated people was frightening on all levels. It was no wonder the boy was little more than skin and bone. Gruff was going to take care of Lyle and nurture him until he was healthy and able to stand on his own two feet. And then, if Lyle would let him, he'd nurture him some more.

But that was a way off yet. Now Gruff tried to lighten the atmosphere by getting everyone involved in cleaning up, including PJ and Jake, who were slinking out of the kitchen.

"Get your asses back in here," Gruff bellowed. He was enjoying this momentary power over his brothers. It wouldn't last, but while it did, he had twenty-eight years of being the youngest brother to make up for.

"It's not my job," Jake muttered, but despite his grumbles he obeyed and started clearing the table.

With eight of them in the kitchen, they all got in each other's way but, for some reason, they really wanted to please Lyle, and by the end of fifteen minutes everything was squared away.

Brad stopped by Gruff before he left the kitchen. He nodded toward Lyle. "Your boy looks tired."

Gruff studied Lyle as he swept the floor, something he had insisted on doing himself. Brad was right. Lyle's face was so pale it was almost gray, making the dark smudges under his eyes look black.

"Time for another nap, boy." Gruff took the broom out of Lyle's hands and handed it to Harry, who protested loudly. Gruff ignored him, sweeping Lyle off his feet, ignoring his squawks and flailing hands.

"What are you doing?"

"Taking you to bed," Gruff said.

"I'm fine," Lyle insisted.

"You'll feel even better after a rest," Gruff assured him.

"I'm not a child," Lyle said with a hint of annoyance in his tone.

Gruff looked down at him, seeing the thin pinched face and huge dark eyes. He looked so much like an annoyed child at this point, yet also a young man out of his depth. "Trust me to know what's best for you, boy. You need a rest. When you wake up, I'll take you on a tour of our land if you want to come."

Lyle's eyes lit up, the irritation fading away. "Just you and me?"

Was that a hint that he'd like to be alone with Gruff, without the entire family joining in? Gruff really hoped so. He took Lyle into his bedroom and, pulling back the comforter, tucked him into bed.

Lyle looked mutinous for a moment, then he sighed, gave the smallest of smiles, and burrowed down under the covers. "I'm a little tired," he admitted.

Gruff bent over and kissed Lyle on the forehead. "Sleep, my boy."

Lyle's eyes went wide. "I like you calling me that. Your boy, I mean."

As if there was any doubt.

"I like calling you my boy," Gruff said.

He brushed his lips over Lyle's, and Lyle closed his eyes.

Gruff straightened and turned to leave the bedroom. Something on the nightstand caught his attention. The note he'd left that morning was still there. How could Lyle have said he hadn't seen it? Gruff frowned. Lyle had lied to him. A cold knot formed in the pit of his stomach. His boy had deliberately lied to him and, he didn't know why.

Troubled, Gruff went downstairs and put on his coat and scarf and gloves. He had a full afternoon's work ahead of him. He would talk to Lyle later. He didn't want to accuse Lyle without knowing the full story. It was just a silly note.

Gruff spent the afternoon doing his usual tasks.

He was splitting logs for a couple of hours. Despite the cold it worked up a good sweat and he took off his jacket and hat, leaving him in his flannel shirt. Gruff rolled up his sleeves and went back to work.

He swung his axe over and over with a rhythm born of long familiarity. It had been his job to provide logs for the fires since he had been a young boy. He remembered being in this very spot with Damien, as his brother taught him how to use an axe. Funny, he had more memories of his brother teaching him chores than he did his parents.

"You must be very strong," Lyle said.

Gruff looked over his shoulder to see Lyle wrapped up in his thin coat and shivering, his lips almost blue. He frowned and hurried over to Lyle. He picked up his own warm jacket, and draped it around Lyle's shoulders, then zipped it up. It reached almost to Lyle's knees.

Lyle looked down at himself and chuckled. "Now I'm zipped up like a mummy. How am I meant to use my hands?"

"Do you need your hands at the moment?" Gruff asked.

"I guess not. If you don't need any help?"

"I'm fine. You sit down." Gruff guided Lyle to a tree stump and helped him sit down. Then he put his fur-lined hat on Lyle's head and went back to work.

He didn't have many more logs to split, and they could have waited, but he liked to get his work finished by the end of the day. When he looked over to see what Lyle was doing, he noticed Lyle's fixed stare on him. He was about to ask if anything was wrong when he saw the high color in Lyle's cheeks.

Oh, someone was horny!

Gruff flexed his arm muscles, and Lyle licked his lips.

Gruff smiled to himself and went back to work, making sure Lyle got a good show. He was very happy to flex his muscles for his boy. It didn't stop him checking Lyle wasn't getting cold, but he seemed content to stay on his tree stump.

When he'd finally finished, Gruff stacked the last logs, put away the axe, and wiped the sweat that had broken out across his forehead, using his handkerchief. He looked at Lyle and wondered what they could do next, then he had an idea.

"I need to wash up and have a coffee. Would you like to go for a ride around our land? It wouldn't be for long because the light will fade, but we could do a quick ride."

"You have horses?" Lyle asked, his eyes lighting up.

"We do. It's the easier way to get around. We have quad bikes, but I prefer to ride my horse. I have an old bay called Maggie. She's been my horse since I was a boy. Do you ride?"

He could have cursed himself when he saw the smile fade from Lyle's face.

Lyle shook his head. "I don't think so. I know I like horses, but I don't think I can ride."

Gruff promised himself that if Lyle stayed with them, he would teach Lyle to ride, and he would get a horse of his own. But at least this afternoon he could get a ride on a horse with him, and Gruff could have the pleasure of holding Lyle close.

Lyle made coffee while Gruff washed up and hunted out an old warm jacket from the chests in the attic. It was one he'd had when he was a boy. It was still too big for Lyle, but from his happy expression he didn't seem to mind. He touched the faded plaid with an odd expression.

"Are you sure? I'll take great care of it."

Gruff wanted to cry. It was a cast-off, a coat Gruff hadn't worn in over fifteen years, yet Lyle treated it as something precious. He also found a hat and gloves for Lyle and then they were ready to go. He held out his gloved hand to Lyle and, without hesitation, Lyle put his hand in Gruff's.

They had about an hour's daylight left, and Gruff considered postponing it until the next day, but Lyle looked so excited, he decided they would take a short ride.

"Harry takes care of the horses," he told Lyle as they walked to the stables. "He's got a real affinity with the animals and always knows if there is a problem. When I was little, he used to try and teach me how to care for the animals, but I didn't have that innate ability to know if there was something wrong. I was very jealous at the time."

Lyle nodded seriously. "The CEO put my friend George in charge of the horses because he had the same ability. Sometimes George would let me help him. Horses are beautiful creatures."

"Something else you've remembered," Gruff said and Lyle looked away.

"I guess it is."

He sounded distraught rather than happy about the idea.

Not sure what to say, Gruff led him to the old barn which housed all their horses.

He introduced each one as they went past, pointing out Damian's stallion Thunder, and he warned Lyle never to say hello to Thunder without Damian being there.

"He's really grumpy," Gruff confided.

Lyle chuckled. "Damien or Thunder?"

"Either. Both." Gruff grinned at him.

It was obvious Lyle would have loved to pat and love on each horse, but night was drawing in, and they didn't have the time. Gruff urged Lyle along to the end stall. He beamed at sight of the rangy old mare. She flicked her ears as if annoyed at being disturbed, but Gruff cooed at her and she came over, nuzzling his pocket because she knew he always had treats in there for her.

"You're a lovely girl," Gruff crooned and stroked her long nose. "This is Lyle. He's going to ride with us today. You show him what a wonderful lady you are."

The look of joy on Lyle's face when he met Maggie made Gruff warm all over. Maggie was a sweet old mare and, really, she was ready to retire, but Gruff hadn't found another horse and, to be honest, he didn't ride that much. PJ and Jake did most of the daily riding as they were responsible for the boundaries of the property. So Gruff kept Maggie, despite his brothers urging him to find another horse.

Maggie gave Lyle a curious look, but she was

happy to accept the treat from Lyle that Gruff had palmed him. Lyle stroked her strong neck and paid her lots of attention.

"Aren't you beautiful, Maggie. Will you let me ride with you this afternoon? I've never been on a horse before, and I'm a little nervous."

Maggie eyed him as though she understood what he was saying, then she looked at Gruff as if to tell him that was okay.

Gruff's heart swelled. Even his horse loved Lyle.

Chapter 5

LYLE

Lyle couldn't believe how lucky he was, as he patted Maggie's strong neck and she twitched her ears, snuffling at his palm as he offered her a treat. He tumbled head over heels in love with her. She was sweet and gentle too, not snatching the treat like some horses did at the theme park. It was easy to see Gruff had trained her right from the start. She was very like Gruff really. Lyle had a sudden mental image of himself naked on his knees before Gruff, who handed him treats for good behavior. Would he become as well-trained as Maggie? His cheeks flamed, and he was glad Gruff wasn't looking at him at that moment. What on earth was he thinking?

Gruff bustled around the barn finding tack for Maggie and grumbling it wasn't where it should be. He returned to Maggie and handed Lyle the tack.

"I'm sorry, it's only going to be a short ride. There's not much daylight left now."

"I don't mind," Lyle assured him, touched by Gruff's consideration.

He didn't want to admit he was extremely nervous at the thought of riding, but he knew he was in safe hands, both from Gruff and Maggie. Gruff allowed him to bridle Maggie, although he watched him carefully and made sure he knew what he was doing. That gave Lyle even more confidence. Gruff took care of him and his horse. But the saddle Gruff brought over made him blanch. It was a huge saddle, just right for the two of them, but there was no way he could get it over Maggie's back. Luckily, Gruff chuckled and settled it on the horse.

Finally, they were ready. Lyle swallowed hard. He could do this. He'd seen people riding before. Gruff taught him how to mount Maggie, although, to be honest, Gruff more or less heaved Lyle onto her. Once he was up on the horse's back, Lyle looked down at Gruff triumphantly.

"I can't believe I'm going to ride a horse."

Gruff grinned at him. "My Maggie will take care of you. You'll love it."

You'll take care of me. Lyle knew, whatever happened, Gruff cared about his welfare. He was still basking in the fact he was actually on a horse. He couldn't believe it. It had been his dream for so long. Gruff handed him his gloves and when he was ready. Gruff mounted behind him. Instinctively Lyles snuggled back against him. Gruff held him close with one arm and took the reins with the other. It became clear quite quickly that the reins were a mere formality. Lyle could feel that Gruff was guiding Maggie by small amounts of pressure from his thighs.

That led Lyle's thoughts down a whole new path, so vivid that Lyle's cheeks flamed, and he was glad Gruff couldn't see him. He was so engrossed at the thought of Gruff around him, guiding him, he didn't realize that Gruff was talking to him.

"Is everything all right, Lyle?" Gruff asked, sounding concerned. His warm breath puffed against Lyle's ear.

"Oh yes." Lyle felt his cheeks heat anew. "I was just thinking about...about...um"

"Things?" Gruff said with a chuckle.

Aware Gruff was mocking him just a little, Lyle decided to say nothing. It was kindly mocking though, and he wasn't offended.

"Things," Lyle agreed.

Like me submitting to you. Like your cock inside me. Like me riding you. Oh God, he was going to spend the whole ride with an erection if he didn't get himself under control. Thankfully Gruff seemed oblivious to his heated thoughts.

Lyle frantically thought of something else to talk about. "Is Gruff your real name?"

Gruff chuckled in his ear. "No, it's Greg. Jake couldn't say Greg when he was little, but he could say Gruff. Everyone started calling me Gruff. When a stranger calls me Greg, my brothers look around, not sure who they're talking about. By the time I was old enough to have a say in the matter, I decided I liked Gruff. I thought it made me sound like a big old bear."

"It suits you," Lyle said.

"Thanks." Gruff held Lyle closer to him and Lyle took the opportunity to lean back against him. "I was going to point out that we've now reached the start of our boundary. I know it's getting dark, but we could make a short tour. If you're not too tired, that is."

Gruff was so thoughtful. He didn't try to make Lyle do anything. Lyle had to admit he found his consideration difficult. He just wasn't used to anyone genuinely concerned for his feelings. The last time anyone had given a care about what Lyle wanted was the day his parents had died. Now, after fourteen years, he was used to accommodating and molding to everyone else. Being asked what he wanted and was it all right actually brought its own stresses, but he didn't want to upset Gruff, so he just nodded, and they carried on walking.

Lyle soon got used to the gentle sway of Maggie underneath him, although he could feel the stretch on his thigh muscles. He was going to have an ache there later on. That made him blush again as he thought of his thighs wrapped around Gruff.

"How do you know this is your boundary?" He asked Gruff the question to distract his thoughts, and because he was curious. As far as he was concerned it was just snow and trees. He couldn't see any sign of a fence.

Gruff chuckled. "I have ridden this boundary my entire life, and I could tell you each tree, each dip in the land that leads us along a line. But there is nothing that actually marks it. We just know."

"Do you have neighbors close by?" Lyle asked.

"No, they are miles away from here, and up at the top is a small boundary with the Kingdom

Mountain." Lyle shivered and Gruff held him close, making a nonsense soothing noise in his ear. "We'll stay away from that boundary," he promised.

Lyle was very grateful. He didn't want to go anywhere near the Kingdom Mountain. At some point he knew he was going to have to tell Gruff that his memory had returned, and he could remember everything that had happened to him in that evil place. But not yet. Now he wanted to rest in Gruff's arms forever and take care of him and his brothers.

Maggie plodded on ahead, as if she had done this every day of her life, which Lyle was sure she probably had. As it grew darker, he started to get cold, which reminded him of stumbling through the snow in the dark the day before.

"It's all right, you're safe with me," Gruff soothed, and Lyle realized he was shaking.

Gruff unzipped his coat to wrap around Lyle. It was like being in a warm, slightly stifling cocoon with Gruff. Lyle didn't care. It drove away the dark thoughts and he was happy to be in Gruff's arms. This was the happiest he'd been in his entire life.

"You're very lucky," he murmured.

"I know," Gruff agreed. "Why do you think I'm lucky?"

"Because of your family and your home. You have people who love you, and you live in a warm comfortable place."

"I am. Even though they drive me batshit crazy, I know they love me and will do anything for me. As I do for them." Gruff's sigh tickled the back of Lyle's neck. "I'm sorry you've been treated so badly, my boy."

"It doesn't matter," Lyle assured him. "You couldn't have known."

You really don't know just how bad it was.

Gruff held him so close he could barely breathe. "It matters to me, Lyle. It matters to my brothers."

Lyle turned to look at him. Under the serene winter moonlight, Gruff's face was a study in planes and shadows. "Why? Why does it matter to you?"

Gruff's opinion was the only one that counted. This prince of a man who'd brought Lyle back to life. Why did he care what happened to Lyle?

GRUFF

The question hung as if it were an icicle in the cold night air between them.

"Why?" Lyle's breath shone white under the moonlight.

Good question. Gruff wasn't sure he could tell Lyle without giving away too much about himself. He could say because he was a decent human being. And no kid deserved to be half-starved by some psycho CEO, whoever he was. And as soon as Lyle remembered who the CEO was, they would find out what it was like to have seven Brenner brothers after them.

And all of that was completely irrelevant to the next words that came out of his mouth.

"I want to be your Daddy."

He heard the hitch of Lyle's breath.

"I'm sorry, you probably don't even know what I'm talking about."

But there was no revulsion, no horror in his expression which was surprisingly clear under the moonlight. Lyle knew exactly what Gruff was asking of him.

"Lyle?"

"Yes?"

"Say something."

Lyle turned his head back to face the way they were going. Maggie kept on with her rolling gait, wending her way through the trees.

"You want me to be your boy."

"I do. I knew I wanted it from the first moment I saw you laying in the snow. Do you know what I mean by being your Daddy?"

"Yes, I do. George told me about Daddies and littles. I don't know how he found out about them. But the minute he told me, it was like something made sense in my head. I've wanted to call you Daddy since I first met you. But..." Lyle let out a long sigh and Gruff's heart sank. "Gruff, there's something you need to know."

"What's that?"

"I haven't, ever, I mean, I've never—"

"Been a boy?" Gruff's excitement grew at the thought of training a complete novice. It didn't matter that he was still a relatively novice Daddy. They could learn together.

"Been with anyone."

The breath caught in Gruff's throat. "You're a virgin?" He could feel Lyle wriggling away from him, trying to put space between them, but being trapped by the coat. "Shh, it's okay, Lyle. It's okay, you don't have to pull away. I was just surprised, is all. I don't mind if you're inexperienced. I've not had a lot of men, myself. I prefer to be in a relationship rather than tomcatting around."

He'd caught the unicorn. A beautiful virgin who wanted to be his boy.

"You don't mind?" Lyle asked and he sounded so unsure.

"I really don't mind," Gruff assured him. "Let's go home so we can talk."

"I need to prepare dinner."

Gruff was about to say he didn't have to do it, but then he thought maybe Lyle would feel better about talking if he had something to keep his hands occupied. Gruff's mom always used to give him something to do if she knew he was troubled and wanted to talk. Usually peeling potatoes. Gruff pulled a face. And for nine of them that was a *lot* of potatoes. By the time he was finished, he'd usually talked out whatever was wrong and just wanted to escape.

"I'll help you," Gruff offered.

"Are you sure?"

"I'm sure, boy."

Lyle's sigh was happy.

They carried on through the cold winter night back to the barn. Lyle seemed deep in thought, and Gruff didn't feel the need to fill the silence with empty chatter.

When they got back to the barn, Harry was feeding the horses. Gruff expected a smart-Aleck crack about Lyle being inside his coat, but Harry took one look at their faces and offered to untack Maggie and settle her for the night. Gruff gripped his shoulder in thanks and promised he would return the favor.

The warmth of the house was a relief after the freezing night air. Even Gruff, who was hardened to it, appreciated the warmth from the crackling log fires. One of the brothers had built up the fires for the evening. Probably Brad. He tended to remember little things like that.

Lyle divested himself of the coat, hat, and gloves, and Gruff showed him where to put them away.

"I don't think I've ever been so warm in my life," Lyle murmured.

The anger built inside Gruff so much, he didn't think. He pulled Lyle against his chest and kissed him. Lyle squawked but it didn't take long for his hands to settle on Gruff's chest and his eyes to close. Even in his anger, Gruff took the greatest of care with him. If this was his boy's first kiss, he wasn't going to let his anger ruin Lyle's experience. He kissed Lyle gently, their lips closed, reassuring him with every touch that this was under Lyle's control. There was time for Griff to be the dominant Daddy. This wasn't it.

He ran his tongue along the seam of Lyle's lips, encouraging him to part them. Lyle opened his mouth and Gruff pressed in gently. Their tongues met, dueled, and parted, only to return and parry once more.

"Get a room," PJ muttered as he walked past.

"We don't need to see you digging for buried treasure."

Gruff ignored him, but PJ had a point. They were in the middle of the hallway. Anyone could walk past. Lyle deserved somewhere private, after their talk. He raised his head and looked down at Lyle who still had his eyes closed. "Hey." He gave Lyle a moment to come back to reality.

Lyle opened his eyes. It took time for him to focus on Gruff's face. "Hey." He sounded breathless.

"Shall we talk later?" Gruff suggested.

Lyle nodded. "That would be good. Should we cook dinner?"

Gruff ran his hand over Lyle's head and cupped his cheek. Lyle leaned into the touch. "You are amazing, boy."

Lyle gave him the most beautiful of smiles. "I'm happy for the first time since my parents died."

"I want to make you happy, boy," Gruff promised.

After just two days Gruff knew he wanted to spend the rest of his life making Lyle happy. He held out his hand, Lyle took it, and they wandered into the kitchen.

Lyle nudged Gruff over to the sink to wash his hands while he looked in the fridge. "I was going to do pot roast, but I won't have time today. I'll do a cottage pie and prepare the pot roast tomorrow."

"What do you want me to do?"

Gruff should really have kept his mouth shut.

"You can peel the potatoes." He raised an

eyebrow as Gruff groaned loudly. "Problem?"

Gruff sighed. "No. Bring it on."

Lyle's smile was sweet. "Thank you."

Gruff sat at the table and looked at the pile of potatoes Lyle heaped in front of him. He was going to be there for a long time.

Chapter 6

LYLE

Lyle hadn't been lying when he said he was the happiest he'd been for a long time. He realized now that living in the Kingdom Mountain had not been living at all. It had been an existence, nothing more than that. He'd had friends, but no one close and no one to call family. Now suddenly he was in a home with seven brothers, and one of them wanted to be his Daddy, and it was almost overwhelming.

Gruff put on his radio, and Lyle heard music for the first time that weren't tunes that the theme park played on endless repeat. Some he liked, some he didn't, but it was new and exciting, especially when Gruff grabbed him and they had an impromptu dance. Lyle couldn't dance, but Gruff didn't mind, and when the music turned slow Gruff held him close and they swayed together.

Later, when Jake and Damien wandered into the kitchen in search of snacks, he discovered the brothers, including Gruff, could sing. They wound up an impromptu chorus, and Lyle clapped so much his hands hurt.

"You're so good."

"Jake's the real star," Gruff said as he sat back down in front of the last few potatoes to peel. "The rest of us can hold a tune but he's the star of the family."

Damien nodded in agreement. "He always was the family show-off."

The three brothers grinned and shoved each other like they were kids, not men in their thirties.

"Why didn't you pursue it as a career?" Lyle asked.

Jake shrugged. "No money. Mom and Dad couldn't pay for lessons. One day I might go back to it, but the family is more important."

Gruff sighed. "It's the same with Harry. We couldn't afford to send him to college to become a vet. And Brad should have been a chemist."

"And you?" Lyle asked. "What should you have been?"

Damien clapped an arm around Gruff's shoulders. "Baby bro would have been a wonderful teacher."

He and Jake vanished leaving Lyle on the verge of tears.

Gruff caught sight of his expression. "It's all right, Lyle. When Mom and Dad passed away, we could have sold up, but by that time we realized we liked it here. All of us had the choice to leave but we decided to stay."

"You don't think of this place as a prison?"

Gruff gave him a huge smile. "Never. It's our castle. We all made a choice to stay here and we've never regretted it. We have our own interests too. Never get near Brad when he says he's going to play in the barn. He's probably going to blow something up." He brought the huge pan of potatoes to the stove. "Okay. What next?"

Lyle couldn't help wishing he'd been born into a family like Gruff's. How different his life would have been. But he hadn't and nothing could change that. He told himself to be grateful for what he had and smiled at Gruff. "Now the ground beef."

They worked side by side until the cottage pie was in the oven, and everything was cleared away.

Brad poked his head around the door. "Smells good. How long?"

"Thirty minutes," Lyle said. "Make sure you're washed up by then."

Brad grunted and vanished.

"I should shower and change before dinner," Gruff said.

"Me too. I smell distinctly horsey." Lyle sniffed his sleeve and grimaced. "Yes, definitely Maggie."

Gruff grinned. "You smell fine to me."

This time Gruff let Lyle walk up the stairs, and they went their separate ways at the top. Lyle stripped off his clothes and went into the bathroom. Having a shower of his own was something Lyle had never experienced before coming here. He still couldn't imagine having his own shower every day. He'd spent years sharing a communal bathroom. Despite his yearning to stay under the hot water, Lyle had a quick wash and returned to the bedroom, just a towel around his waist, anxious not to burn their dinner.

Gruff sat on his bed, dressed only in a T-shirt

and briefs. Lyle smiled at him but Gruff didn't return the smile.

"What's wrong?"

Oh no. What had he done? He'd been so careful but now Gruff was looking at him as if Lyle had personally disappointed him. He couldn't bear it if he'd let the man down and not even realized it.

Lyle's mouth went dry as he realized Gruff held the note. "What?"

"Why did you tell me you hadn't seen the note? You must have seen it because it's unfolded."

"I—" Lyle dried up, unsure what to say.

Gruff gave him a steady look, a deep frown between his thick brows. "You lied to me, Lyle. I don't like lying. If we're going to have a relationship you need to tell me the truth. Why didn't you read the letter?"

Lyle shook his head. "I can't."

"Can't what?"

"I can't read," Lyle said, shame washing over him at the admission.

Gruff's jaw dropped open. "You can't read?"

Lyle shook his head.

"So that's why you didn't read Damien's note."

Lyle nodded, staring down at his bare feet, waiting for Gruff to laugh at him. Would Gruff throw him out now he knew?

"Lyle."

Lyle turned his face away, not wanting to see the disappointment in Gruff's expression.

"Lyle, look at me."

Lyle heard the order in his Daddy's voice and looked up to face him, meeting his gaze. Gruff's expression was hard to read. "I can go. If you take me to the town, I can find work there. Or I can walk."

"You want to leave me...here?" Now Gruff sounded shocked.

"I thought you would want me to leave."

"Why would I do that? Because you can't read?" At Lyle's nod, Gruff said, "Have you never been able to read?"

Lyle bit his lip. He could lie. Just tell Gruff part of the truth. But he didn't want to have his relationship with Gruff be based on a lie. But if he was going to have this conversation, he needed to get dressed. He couldn't be naked while he talked about the events of his life that had led him up to this moment.

"Can I get dressed?" he asked, seeking permission.

Gruff looked a bit taken aback by the question but he nodded. "Sure."

"I want to tell you everything," Lyle said. "But I can't do it naked."

"I'm guessing you want to talk about more than why you can't read?"

Lyle nodded, his hands clasped tightly together, his knuckles white.

"Have you remembered something?" Gruff didn't sound angry, more cautious.

"Can we get dressed first?"

"Okay. Meet me in my bedroom. There's more room in there, and I can hold you on the bed. I'll ask Jake to serve dinner."

You might not want to hold me.

But Gruff vanished and Lyle put on clothes he found on the dresser. They weren't his but they were clean, if a little big. They were obviously one of the brothers' old clothes, judging from the slight musty smell.

He finished dressing and ran a comb through his hair. He stared at himself in the mirror.

"You can do this."

He'd had a little taste of happiness. It was all he could ask for. And he'd hold that close to his heart for the rest of his life.

Lyle left the bedroom, hoping Gruff would be kind to him and not leave him stranded in the woods.

Gruff smiled as he came in. "I was on the verge of sending out a search party to find you." His smile fell away as he saw Lyle's expression. "Why do you look so distraught? The notes don't matter. I don't care that you can't read. It was just a silly note. That's all. I shouldn't have gone so Daddy Bear on you."

"I lied to you," Lyle whispered.

"You were scared. I understand that," Gruff said, obviously not understanding a thing. He held out his hand to Lyle. "Come and sit with me, my boy."

Lyle hesitated but then he climbed onto the bed. Gruff arranged them so they were both comfortable and held Lyle in his arms. Unlike all the other times he'd been in Gruff's arms, Lyle couldn't relax. Would Gruff still want to hold him when he finally confessed everything to him?

"Lyle." Gruff kissed the top of his head.

"Nothing you say is going to make me throw you out. I want to be your Daddy, and that means listening to your problems and helping you if I can."

Lyle relaxed a fraction, but not much. He'd been easier in Gruff's arms when he was half-frozen.

"Lyle, talk to me. Tell me what's bothering you."

The silence seemed to stretch for an eternity. Gruff seemed about to ask again when Lyle spoke in a low voice.

"I've remembered everything."

"Your memory's returned?" Gruff sounded much calmer than he expected.

"Yes."

"That's good, right?"

Lyle shrugged.

"When did it return?"

"It's come back slowly like a jigsaw puzzle," Lyle said. "More and more things slotting into place."

"Like the CEO and cooking for lots of people," Gruff suggested.

"Yes."

"So why don't you tell me what you remember?"

Lyle took a deep breath and blurted out the truth. "I was trapped in Kingdom Mountain theme park for fourteen years."

GRUFF

Gruff heard the words, but they didn't make

sense.

"You worked at the theme park when you were four?"

"No, we started work at eight years old." Lyle sounded so pragmatic about it.

Gruff was horrified. "Lyle, boy, I've got no idea what you're trying to tell me."

He held Lyle closer, and finally Lyle buried his face into Gruff's T-shirt and pressed a kiss over Gruff's heart.

Then Lyle sat up. Gruff let go but captured one of Lyle's hands. He had to be holding him somehow.

"If I tell you, you have to understand that however strange it sounds, I'm telling you the truth. Promise me you'll believe me." Lyle fixed his gaze on Gruff.

Gruff was wary making promises like that, but Lyle was his boy, and how could Lyle trust him with the truth if Gruff refused to believe anything he said?

He squeezed Lyle's hands. "Tell me. You might have to do some talking to get it through my head, but I will believe you."

Lyle hesitated and then nodded. "Fourteen years ago, my parents were killed."

"I'm so sorry." Gruff ached every day for his parents but at least he'd had his brothers. "What happened to them? You don't have to tell me if you don't want to," he added hastily.

Lyle shrugged. "It's okay. It was a long time ago now. We were coming home from visiting my grandparents when we skidded, and the car left the road. My mom and dad were killed instantly. I was lucky I'd been sleeping the back. I don't remember anything about it. I just woke up to discover I was in hospital and my parents were dead. I was alone in the world."

"Oh boy, I am so sorry." Gruff wanted to take Lyle's pain away and all he could say was 'sorry'? "Why didn't you go and live with your grandparents?"

"They rejected me. They made it clear I was too much trouble and they didn't want me, so I ended up in the orphanage."

"You were put in a children's home?"

"I was sent to an orphanage run by the CEO of Kingdom Mountain." Lyle's smile was so bleak it hurt Gruff's heart. "I was four. I didn't know what happened to my mommy and daddy. I thought I was going to a magical place where I'd get my parents back. Instead they shut the gates behind me, and I discovered I was in a prison. The next time I got out of there, I woke up in your forest, and I still don't know how."

"Fourteen years later," Gruff said hoarsely.

"Yes." Lyle's eyes sparkled with unshed tears.

"But... Child Protective Services?"

"Forgot we existed. They never visited. The CEO's influence stretched a long way."

"How many children are in the orphanage?"

"I don't know. I slept with twenty boys in a hut, and there were at least five huts. They moved us around, so we didn't have time to form strong relationships."

"You worked in the kitchens?"

"I did. I didn't mind. I was good at it, and I learned how to cook. But we didn't go to school or learn how to read and write. They said we didn't need to as we worked in the kitchen."

Gruff picked over everything Lyle had told him. "And you helped George with the horses?"

"You have a good memory," Lyle said. "He protected me for a while. Until he reached eighteen and disappeared."

"Oh baby. Why didn't you tell me your memory had returned?"

"Because I was afraid you'd send me back to the orphanage."

Gruff ached for the fact Lyle hadn't trusted him enough, but he understood. Lyle had been betrayed by everyone who should have cared for him.

"You're eighteen now."

"It was my birthday the day you found me."

"Did they tell you that you had to leave?"

Lyle's expression chilled Gruff to the bone. "Worse."

"Tell me."

"When you're eighteen you get offered to the CEO and his team."

Gruff gaped at him. "Offered?"

Lyle nodded.

"And if no one wants you?"

"You disappear," Lyle said, his expression bleak.

"You mean you're allowed to leave?" Gruff knew that wasn't what Lyle meant but he had to ask.

"No."

Gruff wanted to protest. Say this was a ridiculous story. But he'd found the boy frozen in the snow. "No one wanted you?"

"I don't remember," Lyle said. "I guess not. I woke up on my eighteenth birthday and went to work, and that's the last I remember."

Gruff hauled Lyle into his arms and hugged him so tight he heard an "Oof," as the air left Lyle's lungs. "I'm so happy I found you. I hate what's happened to you, but you're my boy and you're welcome to stay as long as you want to. This isn't a prison. If you want to spread your wings and leave, then you can do that too. But you are my boy and as your Daddy, I'm going to take care of you."

"You believe me?" Lyle clung to Gruff, obviously not wanting Gruff to let him go, which was fine with him.

"I believe you, my boy. It sounds unbelievable, but I know evil exists in the world."

What Gruff found hardest to believe was that evil had been on his doorstep all this time and he hadn't known. No one had known.

"I thought I was going to die on my eighteenth birthday, and instead I found you. Well, you found me."

"We found each other." Gruff stroked Lyle's hair, still slightly damp from his shower. "We need to tell my brothers about this."

"I don't want to put them in danger," Lyle said.

"Not knowing could be more dangerous." Gruff cupped Lyle's cheek and raised his head to look at him. "You've got six brothers now who will take care of you, whether they want it or not. You have to tell them."

"They might hate me."

"No, they won't. Trust me," Gruff assured him.

"I do trust you. But I'm scared too."

"Just hold my hand and prepare for the shouting."

Lyle raised an eyebrow. "Shouting?"

"Have you met my brothers?"

Gruff could feel Lyle's hand shaking as they walked down the stairs. "You'll be fine, my boy. I'll be with you all the way."

Harry loped out of the kitchen. "About time. Gruff, I need your help at the stables. Star's got an abscess under her shoe, but she won't let me go near it. She trusts you too."

"She's Alec's horse. Why don't you ask him?"

"He and Jake have gone into town. Business, they said. I think they just want to get laid. But Star's in pain, and I don't want to leave it to the morning. I need an extra pair of hands to steady her."

"I can help," Lyle offered.

Harry smiled at him. "Sure. It shouldn't take long."

Gruff and Lyle quickly scarfed a bowl of cottage pie and headed over to the stable.

"We're gonna smell horsey again," Lyle said.

"That's what showers are for," Gruff said.

"You're very lucky," Lyle told him quietly.

"I know." Gruff wrapped an arm around him. "I

know."

He didn't really know, but he would keep supporting and encouraging Lyle until the boy took the little things for granted too.

They found Harry in the stable, comforting Star. Gruff wasn't surprised he wouldn't wait until Alec returned. He would never leave an animal in pain overnight.

Harry introduced Lyle to Star. The horse whuffled at him and accepted Lyle's caresses.

"You're such a good girl, Star," Lyle told her. "Harry and Gruff are going to make you all better."

Gruff smiled at him fondly.

Harry snorted. "You're so whipped."

"Yup." And he didn't care who knew it.

"Well, keep it in your pants. We've got a horse to fix."

"I think I can keep it under control until we're home," Gruff assured him.

"Could you sound more smug if you tried?" Harry grumbled.

"I'm sure I could try," Gruff drawled.

Harry shook his head, ignoring Gruff's chuckle.

They worked with the ease of long experience, both men content to leave Lyle soothing Star.

Harry grunted when he got the shoe off. "It's a new abscess. It'll heal easily. But I'm going to tear Alec off a strip for not taking care of Star. She won't be going anywhere until it's healed. Thanks for your help, Lyle."

"Any time," Lyle assured him. "I'd love to learn more about taking care of horses."

Harry eyed him speculatively but Gruff pulled

Lyle into his arms. "You can discuss that another time."

"What are we going to do now?" Lyle asked.

Gruff brushed his lips. "Now you have an appointment."

Lyle wrinkled his brow." "I do?"

"Yep. You're my boy, and now I'm going to take you home and make you mine."

"You promise, Daddy?" Lyle asked, sounding breathless.

"For heaven's sake, take him home and screw him through the mattress," Harry grumbled. "Some of us have work to do."

Gruff cupped Lyle's ass, making him squeak. "That's a really good idea. I wish I'd thought of that."

"You're an idiot."

"You're welcome." Gruff gave him a smug grin and swept Lyle out of the barn. It was about time Lyle learned exactly what it meant to be Gruff's boy.

Chapter 7

LYLE

Lyle had never been so pleased to see the log cabin. Turning back to Gruff, Lyle held out his hands to his Daddy. *His Daddy*. He still couldn't believe it. Gruff had claimed him in front of Harry as his. Okay, Gruff had claimed him from the first, according to his brother, but this time Lyle got to hear it.

He was so happy. Gruff beamed at him, putting his gloved hands in Lyle's and letting Lyle tug him up the stoop.

They had things to do. Naked things. And Lyle couldn't wait.

He tumbled into the entry, laughing at Gruff's eagerness, or maybe laughing at his own. He wanted the quiet of their room and his Daddy buried inside him. He shivered at the thought of Gruff entering him, making Lyle his.

He had a home now and it was with Gruff.

"Hello, Lyle."

Lyle turned and his world shattered into a million pieces, each one fracturing his heart.

The CEO of Kingdom Mountain stood in the doorway of the kitchen, smiling at him, his mouth curving as though he were delighted to see Lyle again, but one look into his ice-green eyes exposed the emptiness of his soul.

Lyle gasped and took a step back. Immediately Gruff wrapped his arms around Lyle, holding him tight and anchoring him to the present.

"What's wrong?" Gruff asked, his warm breath ghosting over the shell of Lyle's ear.

Hold me. Don't ever let me go. Don't believe the words that come out of his lying mouth.

"Aren't you going to greet me, boy?" the CEO said.

"Who are you?" Gruff demanded as Lyle shrank back against him.

Damien appeared from the kitchen, his eyes bleak and mouth pinched. "This is David Rogerson, CEO of the Kingdom Mountain theme park. He's here to collect his husband."

"What?" Lyle stared at the CEO in horror. Now he saw a wicked gleam in Rogerson's eyes. "He's not my husband. I'm not married to him. I'm not!"

"I have a marriage license which says different." The CEO held out a piece of paper. Gruff reached around him to take it before Lyle could move.

Gruff studied it and handed it to Lyle who stared at the piece of paper, a numb feeling spreading through him. It was a marriage license for David Stephen Rogerson and Lyle Anthony Parker.

He hadn't even known his name was Parker, let alone that he had a middle name. Lyle closed his eyes, hoping against hope that when he opened them the CEO—he couldn't think of calling the man by his name—and the piece of paper sealing his fate, would be gone. But this time, a miracle didn't happen.

Lyle turned to Gruff and his heart froze at his Daddy's anguished expression. "I didn't know," he whispered. "I don't remember marrying him."

"You pretended not to remember once before," Gruff said sadly.

"I'm afraid my husband has always had a loose relationship with the truth," Rogerson drawled.

"That's not true," Lyle gasped, wrapping his arms around himself. "That's not true!"

"Come on, Lyle, time to go home." Rogerson stepped forward as if he was going to yank Gruff out of his arms.

"That's not my home! I'd rather die than go back to that prison. I've been more at home here than I ever was at the theme park."

Rogerson scoffed and curled his lip. "Don't be so melodramatic, Lyle. You always have such a flair for drama."

"If I'm a liar and a drama queen why did you marry me?" Lyle demanded.

"You asked me, remember? You wanted the richest, most powerful man to take care of you. And that's me."

Gruff narrowed his eyes. "He said that to you, did he?"

"Of course. Rich, powerful, and handsome." Rogerson ticked them off on his fingers. "The full trifecta. Lyle knows where his bread is buttered, and he's a little fire-cracker in bed, but I expect you already know that."

"No. that's not true," Lyle burst out. He'd never been touched by any man except Gruff. Gruff had to believe him. But when he turned to Gruff, he had his whole attention focused on Rogerson. Then he turned to Lyle.

Gruff held out his hand. "Let me see that marriage license again."

Lyle handed it to him and Gruff studied it carefully. "You got married in City Hall."

The CEO's smile grew wider. "Yes, we did. With all our friends there."

Lyle shook his head fiercely. The only people he knew were those he lived and worked with. Kitchen workers and other low-level jobs. He had no friends like Rogerson.

Gruff glanced up from his perusal of the license to fix his attention on Lyle. "Rich, powerful, and handsome. That's what you want?"

"No," Lyle burst out. "I don't care how rich you are, and you're powerful to me. Look at you. You're strong and gorgeous. And you're handsome." Lyle heard Rogerson's snort, but he ignored him, his whole focus on Gruff. He would not let Gruff turn away from him, afraid that if he did that, it would be forever. Lyle wanted to beg Gruff to hold him, but he couldn't take the chance Gruff would reject him. "This man is evil. I don't love him. And I never married him. He's not my husband. He's lying. And I'm a virgin." Lyle felt his cheeks flame, but he was determined to get it out there. "I've never been to bed with anyone until you held me and brought me back to life. We weren't allowed to share beds in the dormitories.

They thought we might form relationships and if we did that, then we'd want to leave."

Gruff's expression didn't change, and Lyle started to lose hope. What did he have to do to convince Gruff that he was telling the truth?

Lyle bent his head. "If you order me to go, I'll go, Daddy. I'm your boy. I'll do what you tell me."

Another snort from Rogerson. "I should have put you on the stage, my boy, instead of in the kitchen."

"He's not your boy," Gruff said icily. "Lyle is *my* boy. Not yours. Because he made that choice. *He* did, not me. Because he's an adult who gets to decide his own destiny. If he wants to stay with me and all my brothers, that's his choice too.

"Unlike you, I don't need to control Lyle. I'll nurture and love him. You take vulnerable children and destroy them. I'm not like that. I may not be rich or powerful, but I'm Lyle's Daddy, because he chose me."

Lyle felt rather than saw Gruff step close to him. Gruff cupped his chin, forcing him to raise his head and look into Gruff's smiling eyes, as warm as the Mediterranean Sea he'd seen in pictures.

"Daddy?" Lyle whispered.

"You're *my* boy. Not his. You're mine. It's obvious he knows nothing about you. And he's lying. Look at the time and date on the marriage license."

Lyle followed his finger. "That's three days ago."

"It's the day we found you." Gruff put his arms

around Lyle. "At four-thirty I was carrying you home through the snow. So how could you be in City Hall marrying Mr. Rogerson here?"

He believes me. He believes me!

Lyle wanted to shriek it out loud. His Daddy believed him.

"You think I'm telling the truth?" he asked, knowing his heart was in his eyes.

"I know you are," Gruff said.

"Give me that," Damien said, taking the marriage license. He studied it, then looked at Rogerson, a deep frown between his thick brows. "I suggest you leave, Mr. Rogerson, before I call the cops."

Rogerson curled his lip. "The sheriff is a good friend of mine. Call me a liar to his face and see what reception you get. I'm very powerful. Cross me and you'll regret it."

Gruff hugged Lyle close to him. Lyle tilted his head to check Gruff was sure, and caught him smirking at Rogerson.

"But I've got the boy. Game, set, and match," Gruff said.

Damien shot him an irritated look. "Not helping, Gruff."

Gruff shrugged. "It's time you left, Rogerson."

The CEO went puce. In the whole time Lyle had known him, he'd never seen anyone say no to him. This had to be a first.

"You'll regret this!" Rogerson spat.

Damien leaned forward and it was almost comical the way Rogerson leaned back, his eyes wide. "Are you threatening my brother?"

"No one takes what's mine," Rogerson snarled.

Lyle couldn't hold back the shiver. He was still scared of the man. Rogerson was rich and powerful, and he could destroy the Brenner family.

Then Gruff turned Lyle in his arms and kissed him, long, deep, and very possessively. Lyle's knees would have buckled if Gruff hadn't held him up.

Rogerson faded from his mind. Lyle was Gruff's. He was definitely Gruff's boy.

GRUFF

Rogerson had gone, leaving behind curses and threats, but Lyle was still in Gruff's arms. Gruff remembered the moment Rogerson had told him Lyle was his husband. He'd have torn Rogerson limb from limb if he hadn't had it fixed firmly in his head that his boy needed him, needed his Daddy. Being locked up wouldn't help Lyle.

Guilt gnawed at Gruff. For one awful moment he'd wondered if Lyle was lying again, just to get out of a bad marriage. When he'd suddenly realized the marriage license was fake. he was ecstatic but also guilty. He should have trusted Lyle. He was going to spend the rest of his life making it up to him.

Gruff had pulled Lyle into his lap. He'd never let him go. They'd been arguing about Rogerson for what felt like hours.

The brothers sat around the kitchen table. Damien had called Alec and Jake, and they'd returned immediately, despite Lyle's protests.

Gruff was glad he'd warned Lyle about the shouting.

PJ was at top volume. "Are you fucking kidding me?"

"Quit cursing," Damien snapped.

"Dollar," Alec and Jake chorused.

PJ cursed again and put two dollars in the jar on the dresser. At a dollar a curse word, they'd soon learned to moderate their language in front of each other.

"I wish I was kidding you," Lyle said, his face pinched. "It's been my life for fourteen years."

"We should raze the theme park to the ground," PJ declared.

"What good will that do?" Harry asked. "Then you've got a hundred or so boys without a home and nowhere to go. No, we bring down the orphanage, but we have to do it properly."

Lyle burrowed deeper into Gruff's embrace.

"It's okay," Gruff whispered. "We just want to help."

"I know you do. But I just want to forget about it."

Gruff rocked Lyle gently.

Damien looked at Lyle, his expression as grim as Gruff had seen him. "This is too important to ignore, Lyle. Every boy deserves the chance to be free."

"We should report him to the sheriff's office," Harry insisted.

"For what?" Damien demanded.

Harry pointed to the piece of paper on the table. "We've got the marriage license."

"Which doesn't prove a thing," Alec pointed out. "He'll deny the whole thing."

Lyle sighed and shifted on Gruff's lap. "Don't underestimate the CEO. He's more ruthless than you could possibly imagine. He will try again. You've got to be prepared for it."

"He can try," PJ muttered, then he winked at Lyle.

Gruff noticed Lyle's worried expression. He brushed his lips against Lyle's temple to comfort him. "What do you think he'll do?"

"I don't know," Lyle admitted. "I was just one of the kitchen boys, but I told you before, kids went missing and didn't return."

"They could have been adopted," Brad suggested.

But Lyle shook his head. "No one got adopted from Kingdom Mountain. We were there to provide unpaid labor for the theme park."

Gruff ached for his boy. He and his brothers had been so lucky with their childhood, compared to Lyle.

Damien frowned, his brows nearly meeting across the bridge of his nose. "What happened when the kids reached eighteen?"

"If they weren't chosen, they disappeared," Lyle said.

"By chosen you mean..."

"Chosen as sex partners for the senior staff," Lyle said bluntly. "And by disappeared, I mean they disappeared from the park, never to be seen again."

All the brothers stared at him. Gruff had heard

it before. It didn't make it easier a second time.

"Disappeared?" Jake said.

"How many people have you found in your woods?"

Gruff buried his face in Lyle's hair. How many boys had he found and left there, not realizing what had happened to them?

"I'm gonna fucking kill him!" PJ banged his fist on the table, sending everything jumping.

Lyle burrowed himself closer to Gruff, who snarled at PJ to get himself under control. PJ glowered at him, but he apologized to Lyle, and put another dollar in the box.

Alec furrowed his brow. "If you were 'disappeared', why did Rogerson try to get you back?"

"I don't know," Lyle admitted.

"I think I do," Gruff said. "Think about it. We find a body in the forest. We let the sheriff know. It didn't happen this time. I bet someone calls Rogerson when the body is retrieved. No phone call this time. He knows Lyle is still alive. Who is the one person who can blow the whistle on the orphanage? He has to get Lyle back."

"But how did he know I was here?" Lyle asked.

"Maybe this visit was just a fishing expedition. Where else could you have gone?"

"And Lyle's right," Damien said. "Rogerson is not the kind of man to take this lying down. He's a nasty piece of work, and he's determined to get Lyle back in his clutches."

"It doesn't help that he's got the cops in his pocket," Brad said.

"I've got friends who work there," Alec said. "I can do some discreet digging. They've got little time for the sheriff, so they won't go running to him."

"I've already got feelers out," Jake said. "I'll let you know what I dig up."

"And I'll take a look at their accounts," Damien said.

Harry snorted. "I'll go take care of the horses. I understand them."

Gruff knew how he felt. He was very grateful to his family, but he had no special skills that could help bring down this evil man. He just needed to take care of his boy.

"I'm tired," Lyle whispered in Gruff's ear.

He sounded defeated, as if he expected to be snatched back to Kingdom Mountain at any moment.

Gruff stood, taking Lyle with him. "We need time alone."

"Is there any dinner left?" Alec asked.

"There's a meatloaf and mashed potatoes already prepared for tomorrow," Lyle said. "You can eat that. I'll make something new."

Alec grinned at him. "I love you." At Gruff's growl, he laughed. "Calm down, big guy. He's all yours. I know."

"We all know," PJ laughed.

Gruff flipped them off and left the kitchen, happy to have Lyle in his arms. He carried Lyle up the stairs to his bedroom. No, their bedroom. He was never spending another night apart from his boy. He kicked open the door and laid Lyle on the bed as if he were precious cargo, which he was.

Lyle sighed as if he were coming home. "There was a moment I thought that was it. I was never gonna know what it was like for you to fuck me."

Gruff shook his head. "I'm not going to fuck you, boy."

"You're not?"

"I'm going to make love to you. When I'm buried inside you, you'll know what it's like to feel your Daddy loving you."

Gruff scooped Lyle into a sitting position and tugged off his sweater, then pushed him down so he could remove his pants, briefs, and socks. He didn't make a show of it. He could do that another time.

Lyle lay back on the bed, his arms over his head, his wrists crossed in the sweetest submissive pose. That was something Gruff would take time to explore. Lyle was lean muscle. Still too thin but so beautiful. He had dark patches of hair under his arms and a treasure trail down his belly leading to tight curls around his half-hard cock. His arms and legs were covered with a faint dusting of hair.

"Gruff, I want to see you," Lyle begged.

"Patience, boy," Gruff ordered.

But he wanted to lay on Lyle, skin-to-skin, his body adoring Lyle's.

He stripped off his clothes, not caring where they fell. He was big and solid, with a furry chest and belly. And a thick, heavy cock which now was hard and leaking in anticipation. Lyle's hungry gaze roamed over him. Gruff stood still, accepting Lyle's admiration. Lyle held out his hand and

Gruff joined him on the bed, laying over him.

"You're perfect, Daddy," Lyle said.

Gruff smiled down at him. "And you were made for me."

The uncertain part of him wanted to ask if Lyle would prefer one of his brothers. They were older and bigger, but Lyle's attention was on him, wanting him. Lyle had never looked at any of his siblings. Gruff wasn't going to spoil this time with uncertainties.

Lyle wrapped his arms around Gruff's neck and his legs around Gruff's waist and pulled Gruff down hard on top of him. Gruff let out a rumbling laugh. For an inexperienced boy, Lyle was a little bossy. Maybe next time Gruff would be more dominant. But for their first time he just wanted Lyle to feel he could ask for what he wanted. He didn't want to instill doubts and fears before he'd had a chance to experience what being loved was like.

Love. Gruff found it hard to believe that he'd fallen in love with Lyle after three days, but there it was. He wanted to spend his entire life making his boy happy.

He pressed his lips to Lyle's, and they parted eagerly under his, allowing their tongues to dance a delicious duet. Lyle arched underneath him, pressing their bodies together and allowing their cocks to slip-slide against each other.

Lyle moaned into his mouth, and Gruff collected the sound and held it as his. He ground his mouth down, and Lyle answered with equal force, running his hands down Gruff's back. Gruff had expected Lyle to be hesitant. However, he was anything but, and Gruff wondered if some of that was to do with the scare they'd both had of losing each other. Neither of them was going to hold back now.

Gruff kissed along Lyle's cheek, along his jawline, and down his neck, then trailed hot, wet kisses over his chest, reaching his nipple. He licked and sucked it, reveling in Lyle's moans of appreciation, before he gave its companion equal attention.

"You taste so sweet, boy," Gruff murmured, raising his head to look down at Lyle's flushed cheeks and glistening lips, his eyes closed and thick lashes fanned out on his cheeks. The abrasion on his left cheek was healing nicely.

"Keep calling me boy," Lyle begged, opening his eyes to stare into Gruff's. "Promise to call me that when we're old."

"You'll be my boy forever," Gruff promised.

"I need you inside me."

"We'll take it slow." Gruff saw the mutinous expression on Lyle's face and gave him a stern look. "I know what's best for you."

He nearly laughed at Lyle's pout but then he wrapped his hand around Lyle's cock and watched the mutinous expression slip away.

"Daddy, more, please more," Lyle cried out.

Gruff jacked him slowly, delighting in Lyle writhing underneath him. A pearl of liquid slid over his fingers, and he bent down to lick it away, getting the first taste of Lyle. He licked around the head and sucked on it, loving the taste of his boy.

He cupped Lyle's ball sac, appreciating the heavy weight of the orbs waiting for their moment. Then he traced one finger backward along the thin skin. Lyle stilled, obviously waiting for what was coming next.

Gruff could have continued with the blowjob, but they both wanted the same thing. He leaned over Lyle and reached into the drawer of the nightstand for the lube and condom.

Lyle grabbed his wrist. "You don't need to use—I mean I've never—"

"But I have and I'm not taking any chances with you," Gruff said. "We'll both get tested."

"You're always thinking of what's best for me. What about you?"

"The joy of being a Daddy is taking care of you," Gruff assured him. "I want to love and nurture you and make you safe. And that includes when we make love."

He saw the joy in Lyle's face, but he saw the tinge of fear too. "What's wrong?"

"What if he comes back for me? What if he brings the cops this time?"

"You're over eighteen, yes?"

Lyle nodded.

"Then there is nothing he can do. You're an adult, and you make your own decisions. And you are safe here."

Gruff fastened his mouth above Lyle's heart and sucked a red mark. "I hold your heart for all time."

Chapter 8

LYLE

Lyle touched the red mark Gruff had left over his heart. It was as if Gruff was kissing his soul. He smiled, wanting to be brave, but he was still scared that the CEO would do something to hurt Gruff and his brothers. They were seven strong men, but Rogerson was powerful and rich, and his influence stretched far beyond the Kingdom Mountain theme park. If he had the sheriff in his pocket, who else did he have who could hurt the Brenners?

"Come back to me, boy," Gruff murmured.

Lyle stared into Gruff's kind, warm eyes, so different from Rogerson's, glacial and hard. How had it taken him so long to see what real men were like, kind and honorable? Rich, powerful, and handsome weren't the perfect trifecta. It was strength of mind, heart, and body which Lyle craved. He cared nothing for power and money.

Gruff caressed his cheek with his thumb. "Where did you go?"

"Nowhere important."

Lyle leaned into Gruff's huge hand. This was Gruff's time. Their time together. Rogerson had no right to intrude on this moment. Lyle encouraged Gruff to kiss him again, to take away his fear with the soft touch of his lips. Gruff did as he asked, but even as Lyle sunk into his kiss, he felt the softest of touches around his hole. He tried not to tense, and Gruff made it easier as he didn't rush, didn't push, just smoothed a slick finger around the muscle until Lyle moaned, needing more. Then he pushed a fingertip in, pressing against the muscle, and out. In and out. Taking his time until Lyle thought he was going to go crazy with wanting more. He begged and pleaded until Gruff took pity on him and pressed in one finger. Lyle breathed deeply. He could handle this. One finger was nothing. Gruff pressed it in deeper and murmured what a wonderful boy he was in his ear.

Lyle accepted the praise and cherished it, made it his, having received so little of it in his lifetime. He was wonderful, he was loved, and he was Gruff's.

One finger became two, and it burned. Lyle was tempted to ask Gruff to stop, and he knew his Daddy would, instantly, but he breathed through it and it got easier. Then Gruff crooked his fingers and Lyle arched off the bed. He grabbed Gruff's wrist, trying to force him back to that wonderful space.

"More," he demanded. "Do it again." Gruff raised his eyebrows and Lyle flushed. "Please, Daddy."

Gruff inclined his head and Lyle was in heaven again.

He discovered he could come just by someone

touching his prostate. Lyle was mortified at the pearly liquid spattering his chest and belly, until he saw Gruff's smug expression. He pouted at Gruff, who laughed.

"You're eighteen, my boy. You'll be hard again soon. I wish I had your recovery time."

Lyle's embarrassment faded as Gruff took his time licking up the come, then investigating under each arm, the soft creases of the tops of his thighs, and the curves of his spine, until Lyle was panting hard, spreading his thighs, and begging Gruff to stick his thick fingers back in his ass. He also learned his Daddy was a tease, tormenting him until Lyle writhed on the end of his fingers and his cock was rock hard again. At some point he realized he now had three fingers inside him, but Gruff had taken his time to prepare him and he'd barely noticed.

"I need you inside me," he begged.

Gruff nodded, and from his frantic expression he was just as desperate. "Just got to get the condom on."

Lyle keened at the emptiness as Gruff withdrew his fingers, but Gruff kissed him and promised they would be joined soon.

He didn't want anything between him and Gruff, but he had a feeling Gruff would stop if he made a fuss. But that testing Gruff mentioned? It would happen real soon.

Gruff nestled between his legs, and the tip of his cock brushed Lyle's hole. Then Gruff pressed, and Lyle sucked in a breath. He felt so full, and it was more than he'd expected, bringing sudden tears to his eyes.

Gruff stopped and kissed the wetness from each eye. "Breathe out, baby boy."

Lyle nodded and forced the air from his lungs. Gruff didn't move. It got easier and then easier still, and Lyle said, "I want all of you."

Gruff slid in to the hilt, and Lyle let out a gasp. He had never imagined it could be like this. That a man would take such good care of him. Gruff leaned over and kissed him. Gruff really liked kissing. Then he moved and Lyle gasped again.

He clung onto Gruff's biceps as Gruff drove him toward a second orgasm. His first climax had taken him by surprise. This one was deliberate, as if Gruff led him every step of the way until they stood at a cliff edge together, looking down at clear blue water.

"Come with me," Gruff said and moved so he brushed Lyle's sweet spot.

Lyle nodded, and they plunged into the ice-cold water together. He heard Gruff yell, but as loud as it was, it was muffled by his own climax.

Gruff hung his head, his arms trembling. Lyle drew him down, ignoring their come-spattered bellies and wrapped his arms around them.

"I ought to move," Gruff mumbled.

"In a minute," Lyle agreed. "In a minute, Daddy."

He never wanted to move from Gruff's arms again.

They cleaned up. Or rather Gruff washed Lyle from head to toe, massaging his scalp until Lyle was a puddle of satiated goo. Even his sensitive cock and balls received a thorough cleaning. Lyle hissed and grumbled but Gruff paid no attention. Then Gruff took a quick shower, not letting Lyle clean him, and they got dressed again, both of them hungry once more.

"I'm sorry if I made too much noise," Lyle said as he pulled a T-shirt over his head.

Gruff looked up from where he was rolling on socks. "Eh?"

"I yelled a lot." Lyle blushed as he remembered.

"I loved you yelling."

"Your brothers might not want to hear me."

Gruff shrugged. "We might be brothers but we're seven gay men living under one roof. Nobody cares if they overhear one of us having sex."

Lyle nodded, not convinced, but trusting Gruff enough not to push it. "Why do you live together?"

"We all work here, and we've never found a reason to move out."

"You don't...uh...together?"

Gruff stared at him. "Me and my brothers? Hell no." He screwed his face up.

"Sorry," Lyle mumbled.

Gruff patted his knee. "You're not the first to ask, and you won't be the last. I'm sure the townsfolk thought we were having incestuous orgies here. But no, we have a farm to run, and we get on fine. It makes sense to live together."

"Do they know you're a Daddy?"

Gruff grinned at him. "We all are."

Lyle's jaw dropped open. "You're all gay Daddies?"

"Now *that* the townsfolk don't know. Seven gay daddies." Gruff stood and stretched, then his stomach rumbled. "Time for dinner."

Lyle shook his head. "I've never eaten so much in my life. I'm gonna be fat."

Gruff scoffed and ran his hand over Lyle's belly. "You were starved before. You need to put on weight, boy. I'm going to make sure you eat enough. Besides..." He patted his stomach. "With the amount of manual labor we do, we don't put on weight. It all goes to muscle."

"I want to help you," Lyle said. "I like taking care of the house and cooking too, but I can help on the farm."

"We'll see," Gruff said. "I'm here to take care of you, not the other way around."

Lyle could see this was going to be a battle of wills. Gruff was stubborn, but he would soon find out Lyle was as obstinate as he was. Lyle had the first taste of freedom in a long time and if he wanted to take care of his Daddy and his family, he would. He just had to work out how to do it without Gruff being aware of it.

They went downstairs. The kitchen was empty, but what was left of the meatloaf and mash waited for them.

"I can't believe they ate nearly the whole meatloaf." Lyle divided the food between them, giving Gruff's the lion's share. At Gruff's scowl he said, "I'm used to eating one small bowl of oatmeal a day. I can't eat as much as you."

Gruff expelled a long breath and stroked his hand over Lyle's hair. "You need to keep reminding me of that. I don't want to make you feel sick."

"You're so kind to me. I worry you're going to get fed up trying to accommodate me all the time."

Gruff furrowed his brows. "Lyle, who made the meatloaf and mash?"

"I did."

"And who made the sandwiches this morning?"

"I did."

"And who made—"

"Okay, I get your point," Lyle interrupted.

Gruff's frown deepened. "You're getting a little bratty."

Lyle hung his head. "I'm sorry, Daddy."

"So you should be," Gruff said sternly, "but I'm not sorry. Do you know why?"

"No, Daddy."

"Because you trust me enough to be your real self." Gruff's frown morphed into a huge smile. "And that's wonderful. Although I'm going to redden your ass if you keep being rude to me."

Lyle flushed with heat at the thought of being over Gruff's knees, his ass stinging with the force of Gruff's hand.

He glanced up to see Gruff studying him closely. Gruff gave him a crooked smile. "Well, that's something to explore for another time."

GRUFF

Gruff whistled happily as he ran down the stairs to cook breakfast. Lyle was still fast asleep on his front, splayed out like a starfish, exhausted after a night of making love and with a beautiful red butt. Gruff had not only found a boy, but one who didn't mind a little kink. He grinned as he thought of the kinks they would explore together. When he'd found a young man frozen in the snow, he'd had no idea the direction his life would turn.

For once, his brothers had left them to sleep. He knew he'd have to catch up with his work later, but he could make it up to them with a cooked breakfast.

Thirty minutes later, Gruff was pulling out eight plates from the kitchen cabinet as someone thumped on the kitchen door.

"That's odd. Most people come to the front door."

He put the plates on the table and went to open the door.

A stranger to him, a sharp-faced thirty-something man in a long, dark-green, wool coat stood outside holding a huge basket of fruit. "Good morning, I have a delivery for Mr. Parker."

Immediately on alert—because Gruff had read the fairy tales too—he shook his head. "Mr. Parker isn't expecting anything."

The man gave a wry smile. "It's in nature of a peace offering from Mr. Rogerson."

Gruff wanted to shut the door in his face, but practicality won out. If the guy was extending an olive branch there was no point chopping it with an axe, and the fruit looked amazing. He took the basket. "Thanks. That's kind of him. I'll pass the message onto Lyle."

Then he shut the door in the man's face.

He put the basket on the side and promptly forgot about it as PJ, Alec, and Harry entered the kitchen, shedding hats, coats, and gloves, and complaining that there was no breakfast on the table.

"It's nearly done," he informed them. "I'm making breakfast this morning. Lyle's still asleep."

"He should be down here making us waffles," PJ grumbled.

"You're spoiling that boy," Alec agreed.

"You've got pancakes, so quit moaning." Gruff ignored the comment about spoiling Lyle. Once they each got their own boy, they'd know what it was like to want to take care of someone special. They probably did know already, but as Gruff's brothers, it was their job to grumble.

He wasn't as good as a cook as Lyle, but he could make oatmeal, pancakes, eggs and bacon without poisoning anyone. Once all the brothers were devouring the food like a pack of ravening wolves, he went up to the bedroom to find Lyle sitting up in bed, blinking sleepily and looking a little confused.

"Hey, there. You were gone, Daddy. What time is it?" Lyle yawned and scratched his belly. "I need to get up and make breakfast."

Gruff leaned over and kissed him. "Already done."

"You're so good to me." Lyle stretched up for a

second kiss. "I can get the laundry started."

"Come downstairs and eat breakfast first." Gruff infused a bit of a growl into his voice because he knew Lyle got turned on by it. Sure enough, he heard the hitch in Lyle's throat. "Up you get, boy."

Lyle got out of bed and stretched. Gruff's gaze roamed eagerly over the boy's naked body, noting the long cock, hard with his morning wood.

Gruff felt his own cock thickening in response but he told himself to get it under control. His boy needed feeding.

Lyle seemed disappointed at Gruff's lack of response, but he obediently got dressed in some old sweats and a hoodie from Gruff's teen years and followed Gruff down the stairs to the kitchen. All the brothers were there, deep in conversation. It died as Gruff entered and he rolled his eyes. "You're talking about me again?"

"You're not that interesting, little brother," Harry scoffed.

"So you're talking about me," Lyle suggested.

PJ leered at him. "You're much more exciting."

Gruff couldn't help the glower, but Lyle just laughed at him. Even under the scowl, Gruff could help the warm glow at the interaction between his boy and his brothers. Lyle had never been afraid of them despite their huge appearances. Some of the men who'd come into the house had virtually run screaming at the sight of PJ's size. Their loss. But Lyle had been different from the start. He really was the boy for Gruff.

"What do you want for breakfast?" he asked

Lyle.

"Just some oatmeal please," Lyle said, sitting down in his usual place.

Gruff served him a bowl and then noticed the basket of fruit. "Do you want an apple with it?"

"Please." Lyle smiled at him.

Gruff selected a bright red apple from the basket and chopped it up. He popped a piece in his mouth as he hunted for a small plate in the cabinet so he could arrange it prettily for his boy. As he stood up, Gruff felt a wave of dizziness sweep over him. He clutched onto the countertop.

"Gruff? Daddy. What's wrong?" Lyle was by his side in an instant, an arm around his waist.

Gruff tried to answer, but his stomach gave an uneasy roll and he had to bend over, breathing through the sudden cramp.

"Quit groping him," Harry laughed.

"Daddy, what's wrong?" Lyle asked, ignoring Harry. "Are you feeling sick?"

"Pain. Stomach," he managed through gritted teeth.

"Was it the apple? Are you allergic?" Lyle reached for the apple, and Gruff swept it out of Lyle's reach. Lyle jumped back, distressed. "Don't touch. Rog...Rogerson. Fruit. Basket."

Damien was on his other side in an instant. "The fruit basket is from Rogerson? Lyle, get the milk."

"Why—?"

"Do it," Damien barked, and Lyle hurried off.

Gruff hated Damien ordering Lyle around like that, but the pain in his belly was overwhelming everything.

Damien forced Gruff over to the sink, Lyle on Gruff's other side.

"What's happened?" Lyle asked worriedly.

"He's been poisoned. Gruff, drink the milk, then you've gotta make yourself sick. Fingers down your throat or I'll do it," Damien ordered.

Gruff could barely hear him as he rode through the cramps, but he got the idea. Lyle helped him gulp the milk even if he did get most of it over the floor. Then he shoved two fingers into his mouth. The results were messy and humiliating, but five minutes later, he hung over the sink, his belly still cramping but empty, Damien and Lyle holding him up.

Finally, he straightened, his legs wobbly like a new-born foal, and wiped his mouth. "I'm okay."

Damien looked at him grimly. "You're not, but you will be. Jake's taking you to hospital."

"I don't need—"

The brothers avoided medical bills at all costs. They couldn't afford a visit to the ER.

"You do," Damien snapped.

Gruff felt too ill to argue. He sat as Lyle got him into a coat and put on his boots, then Damien and PJ hauled him gently into Jake's pick-up, PJ virtually carrying him all the way.

"We'll follow you," PJ said. "Harry and Brad are going to guard the place."

Gruff gritted his teeth and tried to nod. He lay down with his head in Lyle's lap all the way to the hospital, shaking and whimpering. He appreciated Lyle's gentle caresses to his head as he tried to breathe through violent stomach cramps.

If this was what being poisoned was like, it sucked. Big time. It wasn't like this in fairy tales.

Chapter 9

LYLE

Gruff looked almost small in the hospital bed. How had his big strong man been reduced to this by a tiny slice of apple? Lyle stroked Gruff's thick curly hair, not taking his eyes off his Daddy for a second. He was racked with guilt at the thought that Gruff had been poisoned with an apple meant for him, and no matter how the brothers or Gruff tried to convince him otherwise, he knew Gruff would have been fine if he'd never met Lyle.

Damien sat vigil beside him, having replaced Jake earlier in the afternoon. Lyle refused to leave until Gruff did. He hadn't realized as he wasn't a relative, he wasn't entitled to be by Gruff's side, but when they arrived, Jake had done some easy flirting with the charge nurse, who turned out to be Jake's former boy. The nurse promised to leave Lyle alone in return for something. Lyle didn't pay attention, too worried about Gruff, but he did overhear Jake promising to spank the nurse's ass for trying to manipulate him. From the excited shiver the nurse gave, it was a threat he obviously looking forward to.

Gruff was sleeping now. The ER was monitoring him, but thanks to Damien's quick intervention in making him sick, if Gruff's condition didn't deteriorate, he would be released later that day.

"I can't believe the apple was poisoned," Lyle murmured for the hundredth time.

Damien gave him a grim stare. "The whole basket of fruit was poisoned, Lyle. We have a friend who ran tests. Gruff said it was a peace offering? Eternal peace more like. If you'd eaten the whole apple, you'd have been dead. It was a good thing Gruff tried to impress you by cutting it up, and only ate a small slice."

Lyle looked at Gruff, sleeping peacefully in the hospital bed. "I'd never have forgiven myself if he'd died because of me."

To his surprise, Damien squeezed his shoulder. "You are not to blame, you understand? We know who's responsible for this. Hell, he told Gruff. He wants you to know he's got the power to kill you, and he doesn't care who knows it."

"The sheriff's office won't believe us."

"We're working on that," Damien said. "Rogerson is not the only one with contacts. He might be a billionaire, but we are local and known. It counts for something around here."

Lyle took comfort from the grim tone even if it did sound like bravado. He knew Damien would fight tooth and nail to protect his family.

Damien wrapped an arm around Lyle. "I promise you Rogerson will be brought to justice."

"Why are you hugging my boy?"

Lyle looked at the bed to see Gruff scowling at Damien. "You're awake," he said joyfully.

"And you're in my brother's arms."

Damien snorted and pushed Lyle toward the bed. "Keep your panties on. I'm not making a move on your boy who, I might add, hasn't left your side all day."

Lyle let Gruff reel him into his arms. He didn't smell so good, but Lyle didn't care. His Daddy was alive and that was all that mattered.

"How are you feeling?" Lyle whispered.

"Hungry," Gruff admitted, somewhat sheepishly.

Damien unraveled himself from the chair, saying, "I'll go see what you can eat."

"As long as it's not an apple," Gruff insisted.

Damien's lips twitched. "No fruit. I understand."

Once he left, Gruff pulled Lyle in for a hug. "I'm so sorry to have scared you."

Lyle held Gruff close to him. "You saved me. If you hadn't eaten that small piece, I'd have eaten the whole apple and died. Rogerson really wanted me dead."

Gruff stroked Lyle's hair. "I think there's something wrong with him. He could have just let you walk away."

Lyle raised his head. "He knows I wouldn't leave the boys behind, Gruff. If I escaped, he knows that others can escape too. I'm going to make sure of that." He gave a wry smile. "Of course, I'm still not sure how I ended up in your forest, but you saved me."

Gruff looked surprised and then regretful. "We can't save everyone, my boy."

"We have to try, Daddy," Lyle said, staring into Gruff's blue eyes. "How many boys have died because no one gave them a chance? How many years has he been doing this?"

Gruff studied him for a long moment. "Okay. When I get home, we'll investigate how we can save your boys."

Lyle flung his arms around Gruff's neck. "Thank you, Daddy."

Gruff held him close. "I think Snow White had it easier."

Lyle raised his head, his brows furrowed in confusion. "Huh?"

"She ate an apple and fell asleep, to be woken by a kiss from her true love. I got to vomit and spent hours in hospital."

"But your true love was already here, and he didn't leave your side," Lyle pointed out.

"True," Gruff admitted. "Very true."

He encouraged Lyle to rest his head on his chest and Lyle went willingly. They lay like that for a while and Lyle felt sleepy after the trauma of the day. Then Gruff stroked his hair and said, "I called you Snow Twink when I first met you."

"What's a twink?" Lyle asked sleepily.

"It doesn't matter. We'll save that for another time."

"Okay." Lyle was curious but it could wait. For now, he was content to rest.

They returned home late that evening to a raucous reception from his brothers. Lyle stood back as Gruff was passed from one to another for hugs and thumps until he cried uncle and begged to be allowed to go to bed.

Lyle settled him in bed, waited until he was asleep and went back downstairs to find food. He hadn't eaten since the two spoons of oatmeal that morning, but he didn't dare tell Gruff.

Alec and Jake were in the kitchen when he sidled in, unsure of his reception now that he was alone.

Jake grinned at him. "Hey, little brother, you must be hungry."

Lyle stared at him, realizing for the first time he was part of a family. It was overwhelming, and he wanted to run back upstairs to Gruff and cry on his shoulder.

"Lyle? Are you all right?" Alec asked.

Lyle realized he stood in the kitchen doorway, hugging himself. He breathed out and made a conscious effort to relax. "I'm okay. Just hungry. Is there anything to eat?"

"Leftovers in the fridge but you need to start cooking again," Jake grumbled. "None of us can cook as good as you."

"I can do that," Lyle promised. "I'll start tomorrow if Gruff is all right."

He pulled out the remains of a pie and vegetables and stuck them in the microwave.

"We were just discussing how we can investigate Rogerson and Kingdom Mountain without triggering alarms," Jake said.

"I don't know," Lyle admitted. "I can't help you. I worked in the kitchens."

"Do you know who could have delivered the

fruit?" Alec queried.

"From Gruff's description it sounded like one of the green coats, his executive assistants. They all wore the long green coats. We were only allowed to address them as 'sir'. I don't know his name." The microwave beeped, and Lyle pulled the plate out. "I didn't know my full name until he tried to fake our marriage. He might have lied about that too." The thought had just occurred to him.

Alec hummed and tapped his chin. "We need to make a visit to Kingdom Mountain."

Lyle stared at him. "You can't go there."

"Why not?"

"Do you know how many things could go wrong? He could kill you with a drink or an accident on a ride. You can't go there."

"He doesn't know what we all look like," Jake pointed out.

Lyle banged his plate down on the table and sat down opposite him instead of in his usual space, scowling fiercely. "This is not a game, Jake."

Jake looked at Alec and then back to him. "I know it's not a game. But we need to get in there or we'll never know what's going on."

"You all look like Gruff," Lyle said. "Even Harry. You're just bigger versions of each other."

Jake smirked at him. "Believe it or not, I know how to disguise myself. Don't you worry, little bro."

Lyle shook his head. "If something happened to you, I'd never forgive myself."

Alec looked at him, and for the first time, Lyle

saw a core of steel running through him. "Jake and I have done this before. If we say we can infiltrate Kingdom Mountain, then we can. We just need the intel from you."

Lyle stabbed at the food on his plate. They had no idea what they were up against. He might not be able to physically stop them, but he would tell them fourteen years' worth of information. He might be able to put them to sleep from information overload.

GRUFF

Gruff stirred back to consciousness and cracked open one eye to discover it was still dark and Lyle wasn't in his bed. He sat up and his stomach gave an uneasy roll, but he thought that was more to do with it being empty than being poisoned. Gruff was used to eating huge meals and snacks. At the moment though, he was more concerned about the empty half of his bed. He switched on the lamp on his nightstand to see the pillow undented by his boy's head. Lyle obviously hadn't come to bed at all.

Where was his boy?

He peered at the clock. 3:05.

Worry coursed through him. No one had woken him up to tell him there was an issue. Gruff pushed back the covers and stood, swaying a little before his head and his feet caught up with each other. It was chilly in his room and he shivered, grabbing his robe from the back of his door and wrapping it around himself before going outside to discover the cabin still lit. He heard voices from the kitchen. What on earth was going on?

"So the kids are dropped off all the time?" Alec asked as Gruff walked into the kitchen to discover his entire family, including Lyle sitting around the table.

"Yes, one or two every few months to replace those who leave. Although less in recent years," Lyle said. He looked up at Gruff and sprang to his feet. "Daddy! Are you all right? Do you need anything?"

Gruff took him into his arms, noting how tired he looked, his eyes dull instead of their usual warm brown. He stroked Lyle's hair, and Lyle leaned into the touch. "I needed you, my boy, but you weren't in our bed."

"It's our fault, baby bro," Alec said. "Your boy here was telling us about the set-up at the theme park."

"It's three in the morning," Gruff pointed out. "He needs his sleep."

Lyle slumped against him. "It's not your brothers' fault. There was a lot to talk about."

Gruff put a finger under Lyle's chin and tilted his head to look into Lyle's eyes. "You should have woken me up."

"You needed sleep," Lyle whispered.

"I needed you more." Gruff added a growl to his voice to let Lyle know he was annoyed, but it wasn't irreparable.

Lyle shivered as he always did when Gruff growled and buried his head against Gruff's chest, obviously seeking comfort. Gruff held him close and looked over his head at his brothers.

"You should have woken me up to be here for my boy. I needed to hear this too."

To his surprise most of them nodded, and Damien said, "I'm sorry. You're right. You're Lyle's Daddy. You should have been here."

Whoa. Gruff did his best to keep the shock off his face, but it wasn't every day his older brothers apologized. He was tempted to ask if they could run that again and he could record it, for posterity. But then his stomach growled, and Lyle raised his head.

"Are you hungry?"

"Starving," he confessed.

"Me too," PJ added.

And the chorus of agreement around the table made Gruff roll his eyes.

"I'll make waffles," Lyle suggested.

"And bacon?" Gruff asked hopefully.

"Eggs too if you want." Lyle furrowed his brow. "We going to need more groceries."

"That's PJ's job," Harry said. He got to his feet and headed for the pantry. "I'll help you, Lyle. Alec and Jake can bring Gruff up to speed."

"I'll go with you to the grocery store," Lyle said to PJ. "I'll make a list."

PJ sat back with a grin on his face. "You picked the right boy for us, little bro."

Gruff pulled Lyle back into his arms and glowered at PJ. He wasn't going to let his brothers take advantage of his beautiful boy. "I picked the right boy for *me*. He's mine, not yours."

"I like doing this," Lyle said anxiously.

"I know, but we've never had a boy who

belonged to us. You're special."

"And you can cook," PJ said. "That's a first."

Damien burst out laughing. "Do you remember that kid you brought home, Alec? What was his name? Matt! That was it. He nearly burned down the cabin when he tried to make you toast."

Gruff chuckled along with his brothers but he noticed Alec's seemed a little forced. He'd always had a feeling Alec had been more interested in Matt than he'd let on. Matt was a free spirit and hadn't wanted to be tied down with one Daddy.

"I had a friend like that," Lyle chuckled. "George was useless in the kitchen, but he was really good with horses."

"I'd be happy to find myself a boy who loved working with the horses," Harry said as he came back into the kitchen, laden with food.

Gruff's stomach growled just at the sight of the food. "Could we eat it now and cook it later? I'm so hungry."

Lyle smiled at him. "Bread and butter to stave off the wolves?"

"Perfect. And hot chocolate?"

"Done."

Gruff sat down where Lyle had been. He didn't want to admit it, but he was glad to sit as his legs had been feeling wobbly. He looked around the table at his brothers. "Where do we start?"

Jake glanced at Alec and then at Lyle who was busy pouring hot chocolate into a cup. "Lyle's told us how the kids lived, and it's grim. They were there as cheap labor, and no one cared about them. No one even checked on them."

Gruff's heart ached for Lyle and all the other children abandoned by the system. He accepted the cup from Lyle with a murmured thank you and a pat on Lyle's butt. "We've got to get them out of there."

Alec tapped his fingers on the table. "We can't just walk in and say, 'Hand over the kids.' And then what do we do with them? We can't take on a hundred children."

"We could get the authorities involved," Gruff suggested.

"Who would listen?" Lyle said, as he placed a wooden board with an entire loaf sliced and buttered in front of them. "It was the authorities that left us there. Daddy, you go first as you didn't get dinner. Oh, don't look like that, PJ. I know what you ate for dinner and then a midnight snack. Besides, there's another loaf in the oven."

Gruff grinned at the outraged look on PJ's face as he filled a plate with bread. It was good to have someone who had his back. But he sobered quickly when Brad said, "I don't care if we turn into a giant kids' home, we're getting them out of there."

Lyle gave them all a wistful smile. "When I first arrived at the theme park, I used to dream of someone rescuing us like in the fairy tales. I soon realized there wasn't a fairy godmother for boys like me."

Gruff held out his hand and Lyle came over to him. "I'm sorry you had to wait for me."

Lyle's eyes glittered. "You were worth waiting for."

"If this gets any more schmaltzy, I'm gonna hurl," PJ muttered.

"Been there, done that," Gruff said smugly. "Got the hospital bill to prove it."

Lyle gasped as PJ made a gagging noise.

"Who's making this breakfast?" Harry grumbled.

Lyle hurried over to the stove while Gruff dived into the bread and listened to Alec talk about the theme park.

"Jake and I are going there to scout around," Alec said.

Gruff nodded as his mouth was full. "When?"

"Soon." Alec's expression turned grim. "Rogerson understands we all know about the orphanage and what he's been doing to the kids. He's got two choices, and neither of them are good."

Gruff didn't need to hear Alec spell it out. David Rogerson was a caged animal, and he would lash out. He also thought he was invincible, and no one could bring him down. His arrogance would be his undoing.

"You and Jake be careful," he said finally.

Alec beamed at him. "We always are, baby bro."

"You're not encouraging him with this crazy idea, are you?" Damien said.

Gruff shrugged. "What choice do we have? We need information. He didn't get to be the CEO by being stupid. Alec and Jake know what they're doing. You know they've been doing work like this for years. They just think we don't know. Maybe they're not so clever."

Jake growled, but he was grinning at the same time. He threw a piece of bread in Gruff's direction. Gruff caught it and popped it in his mouth.

Damien threw his hands up in the air. For a moment he looked so like their father. Gruff looked down at the table so no one caught the sudden tears in his eyes.

"So you guys stake out the theme park," he said, hoping his voice didn't sounded as raspy as it did to him. "Then what happens?" He looked up to see Alec's evil grin.

"Then we set a trap to catch a rat."

Chapter 10

LYLE

Lyle expected to start the day's chores after breakfast, but Gruff hauled him into his arms and told him they were all getting sleep, including Lyle.

Damien nodded and yawned. "We'll start the day at ten. We've got a delivery of trees and logs to the town. Lyle, if you want to come with me and PJ, we can get food supplies too."

Lyle looked at Gruff for permission.

Gruff looked disappointed but he said, "It's a good idea. I can start on the trees on the west side."

"I'll help you once I've checked on Star," Harry said, scowling at Alec, who looked guilty.

"I'm sorry. I never meant to cause her pain."

Harry growled and brushed past him to go up the stairs.

"He knows you didn't mean it," Lyle assured him.

Alec patted Lyle's arm. "I know. Harry's got a huge heart where the horses are concerned."

"Okay, time for bed." Gruff yawned in Lyle's ear. "Before I fall asleep standing here."

Lyle wrapped his arms around Gruff's neck.

"Take me to bed, Daddy."

Gruff waited.

"Please, Daddy."

Gruff gave a pleased growl and headed up the stairs and into his room.

Lyle shed his clothes wearily and climbed into bed next to Gruff. He snuggled next to him and laid his head on Gruff's furry chest, which was fast becoming his favorite pillow.

"My brothers really like you," Gruff said, which was more of a rumble above him.

"I like them. I like taking care of them too."

Lyle yawned, inhaled the woodsy scent of Gruff, and closed his eyes. "G'night, Daddy."

He was asleep before he heard if Gruff responded.

Lyle woke feeling warm and cozy, and hard enough to drill through the mattress. He stretched and sighed happily. For once when he opened his eyes it was light in the room. Then he remembered it had been nearly five before he'd gotten to bed.

He yelped as something warm and wet licked across his tip of his cock. He looked down to see Gruff settled between his legs and feasting on his cock.

"What are you doing?" Lyle squeaked.

Gruff looked up, his eyes sparkling. "Giving you your first blowjob."

"I've never—"

"I know. Lay back and let me give you the best good morning ever."

"I should be taking care of you, not the other way around," Lyle insisted.

"And you will, my boy. I'm going to teach you. But first, you can enjoy this one."

Lyle tangled his fingers in Gruff's thick hair. Not to push. Never that. But he wanted to feel the rhythm of his Daddy pleasuring him.

Gruff pushed Lyle's legs up, and sucked on his balls, rolling the delicate orbs with his tongue.

Lyle moaned, biting down on his lip. "Please."

"Please what?"

"I need to come, Daddy, please."

"Not yet." Gruff's voice was stern but his eyes had a wicked twinkle.

Oh, his Daddy was enjoying this. Lyle wanted to wriggle with joy, but Gruff's hands held his hips in a tight grip. He had to stay still and think about all the horrible things he could to stave off his climax. But inexorably Gruff's hot mouth his cock drove him closer to his climax.

"Daddy!" It was almost a scream.

"Come for me, boy."

Lyle thrust up, and Gruff took him to the hilt, his nose buried in Lyle's pubes. Lyle's balls tightened and he came with a strangled cry, Gruff taking every drop. When he'd finally emptied himself down Gruff's throat, Lyle collapsed back on the bed, staring up at the ceiling.

Gruff gave his cock one last kiss and crawled up the bed beside him, laying his large hand on Lyle's belly.

"That was..." Lyle ran out of words.

Gruff chuckled and leaned over to kiss Lyle on

the mouth. "I'm glad that was."

Lyle turned to face him. "What about you?"

"This one was just for you, boy. You can practice on me later."

Lyle furrowed his brow, not happy that his Daddy had to wait but Gruff smoothed away the lines.

"I like taking care of my boy," Gruff said, "and speaking of taking care, you need to have a shower."

Lyle was ready for more sleep, but he nodded and wearily climbed out of bed to go into the bathroom. Gruff followed him in and turned on the shower, encouraging Lyle to get under the hot water. Lyle squeaked as Gruff climbed into the shower with him.

"I'm going to take care of you every day," Gruff informed him, "and that includes washing you."

"I can wash myself," Lyle said timidly. "You don't have to."

Gruff growled a little, and Lyle jumped. "I know I don't have to, but I'm going to take care of every day. Because you're my boy, and I want to."

He reached over and picked up a bottle. Lyle looked anxiously, but it wasn't a Kingdom Mountain bottle and he relaxed.

Gruff followed his gaze. "There are no Kingdom Mountain bottles in the house. Brad went through everything yesterday. They're all in the trash."

"Thank you."

They were all so good to him. Lyle would thank Brad with his favorite meal.

"Put your head back in the water, and I'll wash it," Gruff ordered.

Lyle sighed as strong fingers massaged shampoo through his hair. This felt amazing. By the time Gruff had washed his hair and soaped his body, Lyle was purring.

If he could have this every day, he'd be so happy.

An hour later, Lyle climbed into the truck next to Damien. He was a bit nervous of sitting with Gruff's eldest brother, but PJ had gone ahead with the Christmas trees. They had the trailer packed with seasoned logs.

"Ready?" Damien asked.

"Ready."

Lyle waved to Gruff as the truck pulled away from the cabin. He couldn't help the nerves fluttering through his belly. This was the first time he'd been away from the house, and he wasn't with Gruff. But it was also exciting. This was his first time seeing the world away from the mountain. Gruff had assured him the town was small and not particularly interesting, but Lyle had nothing to compare it against. It wasn't Kingdom Mountain, and that was all he could think about.

Lyle was so lost in his thoughts; it hadn't occurred to him that Damien was quiet too. Then Damien said, "I've never seen my brother fall for a boy so quickly."

Was that a compliment or a criticism? Lyle wasn't sure. He glanced at Damien but couldn't read his expression as he drove.

"I feel the same way about him," he confessed.

"I can see that."

"You don't like it?" Lyle hated the thought that Damien disapproved but it was better to know.

"I wasn't sure at first," Damien confessed, "but the more I get to know you, the more I realize you're just right for my little brother."

"But?" Even with the compliment there was definitely a 'but' in Damien's voice.

Damien sighed. "You know nothing about the world, Lyle. What's happens if you decide you want a big adventure away from here?"

"Are you worried about me taking Gruff away from you?"

"Maybe." Damien turned to look at Lyle briefly and then back to the road. "I know we can't all stay together forever."

Lyle stared out at the narrow mountain road as he thought about what to say. It was kind of unfair to blame him for what Gruff may or may not do in the future.

There was a sharp bend coming up. He thought Damien was approaching it too fast.

"Damien?" he said in alarm, when the truck didn't slow.

"We've got no brakes," Damien said grimly.

Tension flooded through Lyle. If they didn't slow down, if they didn't make that bend, they would go over the edge.

As they approached the bend a van zipped around the corner on their side of the road.

Damien swerved, heading for the mountain.

Lyle braced himself for impact. He heard the screech of brakes, and Damien's yell. Then everything went black.

Lyle groaned. He opened his eyes, squinting because his head hurt. He was at an odd angle.

A face appeared in field of vision.

"Good morning, Lyle!" the CEO said.

Fear took Lyle back into the darkness.

GRUFF

Gruff took a deep breath, inhaling the scent of pine and crisp snow overlaying the rich dirt beneath. Beneath him, Maggie moved with the rolling gait of a horse who knew where she was going and didn't need her rider to guide her.

He missed Lyle in his arms like an ache, but it would be good for Lyle to spend time away from the farm and away from him. No matter what Lyle said, Gruff hated the thought that Lyle would go from loving him to feeling trapped in another prison. They barely knew each other, yet Gruff felt Lyle had lodged in his heart like a seed taken root. In the short time, Lyle had unfurled like new leaves seeking the sun. Gruff wanted to nurture Lyle until he was strong and confident. But was that what Lyle needed? Did he need Gruff, or did he need to get far away from here and start a new life with no chance of being discovered by Rogerson or his goons.

Gruff had no idea what the best decision for Lyle was, but he did know if Lyle wanted to leave, Gruff would let him go. If he'd been taught anything by his big brothers, it was when to let a boy spread his wings.

Maggie clopped along under the early winter sun and they reached the clearing where his brothers had stopped chopping down this year's trees. It was time to get them harvested and ready for sale. Despite their reputation, the towns folk always bought their Christmas trees from the Brenner boys, and the brothers always donated a tree to put up in the town square as their parents had. Life hadn't really changed that much.

"Okay, Maggie. Time to work."

He was about to dismount when his phone vibrated, which reminded him he was going to have to get Lyle a phone.

He looked at the screen. PJ.

"Hi, PJ."

"Gruff, have you heard from Damien?"

Fear sent its icy tendrils through Gruff. "No. What's happened?"

"Someone cut the brakes on Damien's truck, and Lyle is missing."

Gruff was going to pass out. He couldn't breathe. No air in his lungs.

"Get it together, baby bro," PJ snapped. "He needs you to think with your upstairs brain."

Gruff forced in a shaky breath. "I'm okay. I'm okay."

"Good. Now listen. Damien came round as they were dragging Lyle away. Rogerson's got him. It was a Kingdom Mountain van. Harry's coming to get you."

"No," Gruff said. "It'll be quicker if I ride

Maggie up there from here."

"You can't go there on your own."

"I have to. I can't wait for Harry."

"No, Gruff, wait—"

Gruff disconnected the call. All he could think about was reaching Lyle before Rogerson had the chance to make him disappear again. Was Lyle hurt? How would he get to Kingdom Mountain? Question after question tumbled through his mind. His phone vibrated. Stopped. Vibrated again. He knew his brothers would keep calling him. Gruff was tempted to switch it off but he might need someone to track him if things went wrong. Or he might need to call someone in a hurry. He compromised by putting his phone on silent.

"Maggie, old girl, we need to get to Kingdom Mountain."

Maggie looked over her shoulder as if to tell him she understood, and he urged her forward. But the higher up the mountain they traveled, the worse the snow became. It was dangerous for Maggie and the last thing he wanted to do was put her at risk.

"We're going to head for the road," he told her.

She huffed in agreement, and Gruff picked his way gingerly to the road that led up to Kingdom Mountain.

All he could focus on was his boy. Lyle needed him and he was going to rescue him no matter what. If the sheriff arrested him then he'd have to plead his case, but he wasn't leaving his boy in the hands of that evil man.

They reached the road, and Gruff took stock of his surroundings. He'd never been to Kingdom Mountain, and the road was too twisty to work out how close he was to the theme park. He edged closer and looked down the mountain, squinting at the town which nestled in the valley far below, which was where Damien and Lyle had been heading. How far down the mountain had they gotten before Damien realized the brakes didn't work?

As he studied the road, he noticed a green van making its way up the mountain. He stared at it idly for a moment and then closer. A germ of an idea sprung into his mind.

Gruff looked over down his horse. "Maggie, we've got to hijack a van."

Maggie neighed as if in agreement.

Chapter 11

LYLE

Consciousness didn't come easy to Lyle. He groaned as pain shot through his head. It wasn't helped by the constant motion. He must be in a vehicle. Was he in an ambulance? What had happened? The brakes! The truck! He remembered the slide into the tree. Damien!

Lyle opened his eyes. He was lying on the floor of a van.

"Hello again, Lyle."

David Rogerson turned in the front seat, giving him a thin smile, his cold eyes boring into Lyle.

His heart pounding, Lyle scuttled away until he was against the side of the van. "What do you want? Why am I here?"

"I would have thought that was obvious. I want you."

"No. Leave me alone. I'm not yours."

Rogerson gave him a smile that chilled Lyle to his bones. "You are mine. You were mine since the day you arrived at Kingdom Mountain."

"No. I'm eighteen. You didn't pick me. You disappeared me."

"My mistake. Now you're coming back to my apartment."

"No. I'm Gruff's. Not yours."

"Oh yes, the little woodsman."

"He's my Dad—"

Rogerson's lip curled. "He's my Dad—? Daddy? How funny that you think this man is your Daddy. Don't worry. You'll soon find out what it's like to live with a dominant man."

Fear flooded Lyle. "No!"

"You seem to think you have a choice, my boy."

"I'm not your boy." Lyle drew his knees up to his chest and wrapped his arms around his legs. "Let me go. Just let me go. I won't say anything."

The laugh Rogerson gave chilled Lyle to the bone. "You must be very naïve, my boy, if you think I believe that."

"We'll be there in ten minutes, sir."

Lyle realized he knew the voice. It was Hunter. He was a strange man that had worked at the theme park. Lyle was never sure exactly what he did.

"Drive straight to the castle," Rogerson barked.

"Yes sir."

Rogerson seemed to lose interest in him and turned back to face the road.

Lyle took a deep breath. He needed to find a way to rescue himself. Who knew what had happened to Damien. *Please, please, let Damien be all right*. He'd never forgive himself if Gruff's brother died because him. His breath caught in his throat. Gruff probably didn't even know he was in trouble yet.

"What on earth?" Hunter muttered.

"What's the matter?" Lyle asked. His heart leapt at the possibility of rescue, only to fade when Hunter spoke again.

"There's a horse in the middle of the road," Hunter said.

"Go around it," Rogerson ordered.

Hunter slowed to a crawl and attempted to ease around the bay horse who stood calmly watching them. Hunter cursed as the animal got in his way again.

"I'm going to have to move it," he said.

Lyle blinked at the sight of the animal.

Is that Maggie?

Even as he thought that the van door opened and Gruff scrambled in. Lyle's heart thudded in relief.

"Gruff."

Gruff's attention was focused solely on him. "Are you all right, my boy?"

Lyle launched himself at Gruff, thrilled to be in his arms.

"Take me home, Daddy. Please take me home."

"I don't think so," Rogerson turned in the front seat and aimed a gun at them.

Lyle shrank back in Gruff's arms.

"Don't be stupid, Rogerson," Gruff said. "Just let us get out of here."

"You and your sweet boy. You both seem to think I was born yesterday. Shut the doors now."

Gruff leaned forward and closed the doors, not letting go of Lyle for a moment.

The gun didn't waver as Rogerson ordered, "Hunter, take us further up the mountain."

The van engine roared as it picked up speed. Not being able to see was disconcerting. Especially as Lyle knew they were careering up a narrow road. He prayed that nothing was coming the other way. Hunter wasn't going to slow down for anyone.

"What will happen to Maggie?" he whispered to Gruff.

"She'll go home." Gruff sounded confident although Lyle could see the worry in his eyes.

"Stop talking," Rogerson ordered.

"What are you going to do with us?" Lyle couldn't control the quaver in his voice.

"Well, I've changed my mind about taking you as my boy. You're too much trouble, Lyle. There's a ravine coming up. They'll never find either of you there."

"You're going to kill us?" Gruff pulled Lyle closer into him as if he could protect him by the size of his body.

"No, Mr. Brenner. Hunter is going to kill you." Rogerson gave them a wicked smile which chilled Lyle to the bone. "I rarely do my own dirty work, and with the trouble you've given me I remember why."

"My brothers will find us. They know it's you trying to kill us."

"But they'll have no proof and without proof, you were just a boy trying to break back into Kingdom Mountain, along with his really aggravating boyfriend. We'll put your bodies into the van, set it alight and push you off the edge of the road.

Lyle shook as he heard Rogerson describe his death so calmly. "I'll come with you if you let Gruff go."

"What?" Gruff roared. "No. No way."

"Nice try, Lyle. But it isn't going to happen. You don't have to play the martyr and sacrifice yourself for your boyfriend."

"I would do anything for him."

"Yes, I believe you would. Strange, I have all the power and wealth and yet you pick him. Why?"

He sounded genuinely curious.

"Look in a mirror, dude," Gruff muttered.

"Mirror, mirror, on the wall. Which man has it all?" Rogerson mocked.

Gruff kissed the top of Lyle's head. "I think that would be me."

Lyle raised his head to kiss him. "I love you, Daddy."

Rogerson's jaw dropped as if he could believe Lyle hadn't picked him, then his expression hardened. "I'm going to kill you now."

He aimed the gun at Lyle.

Suddenly Hunter knocked his arm upward. "No! No more killing. I won't murder for you again."

But the van swerved. Hunter had to fight to control the steering. Enraged, Rogerson brought the gun down and fired at Hunter.

The sound was deafening in the confined space.

GRUFF

With Rogerson's attention elsewhere Gruff

kicked at the lock. It didn't give. He kicked at it again and this time the doors flew open.

The van lurched as Hunter slumped over the wheel, a large red stain spreading over his jacket. The van picked up speed as it swung wildly, and Rogerson cursed trying to push Hunter's body away from the wheel. His efforts were futile.

Lyle clung onto Gruff, his gaze locked on Gruff's. It was clear he knew as well as Gruff their chances of surviving this were slim.

No time to focus on Rogerson. Gruff looked out of the van. They were heading for the next corner. Too fast. Rogerson couldn't control the van. There was only one thing he could do to save Lyle, but he had to be quick.

Gruff hung onto the strap and looked out the van. He looked down at Lyle's frightened face. "I'll always love you, my boy."

Then he threw Lyle out of the van. Lyle had no time to say anything as he shrieked and landed on the road. Gruff didn't even have time to see if he was all right.

The van dipped. His time had run out. He launched himself out the back as the van went over the edge. Gruff heard Rogerson scream as he slammed into the mountain side, his hands and feet scrabbling to get purchase. By some miracle he managed to grab the root of an old tree, but it bowed under his weight. It wasn't going to be able to hold him. As his hands slipped, he closed his eyes, hoping the fall would be quick. He heard the van crashing down the mountainside and Rogerson's scream cut off abruptly.

Then he was hauled up by two strong hands under his armpits. He collapsed onto the road and lay sprawled out, gasping for air. Someone rolled him over and he saw PJ, Alec and Jake staring down at him, all of them white and shaking.

"Gruff, are you all right? Talk to us, baby bro," PJ demanded.

He tried to speak but his mouth wouldn't work. Finally, he managed to put a sentence together. "Where...did you come from?"

"We were following you. You just didn't see us. I nearly ran over your horse and then your boy."

"Lyle? Is he—?" He tried to raise his head, but Jake pushed him down.

"Lyle's fine apart from a sprained wrist."

"Where is he?"

"He fainted when he saw you go out over the edge," PJ said. "Jake checked him. He'll be fine when he wakes up."

"Rogerson?"

"Spread over the ravine, I hope," Alec said with grim satisfaction.

Gruff slapped away the hands trying to keep him down as he sat up. He ignored their grumbles. He had to see Lyle. He tried to stand but his legs refused to work.

"Stay there," Alec said. "We'll bring him to you."

But nobody was going to put his hands on Gruff's boy. He crawled over to where Lyle was sprawled unmoving on the road, leaving his brothers muttering behind him.

Lyle's left wrist was already puffy, and he had

abrasions and road rash over his face and hands, but he was alive. That was all Gruff cared about. He sat by Lyle, tears prickling his eyes. If he hadn't thrown Lyle, he wouldn't be hurt like this.

"My boy, I'm so sorry."

He bent and brushed his lips over Lyle's mouth, then gave him a deeper kiss. Lyle moaned and kissed him in return, then his eyes flew open.

"Daddy?" Lyle sat up, almost headbutting Gruff in the process. "But I saw you go over the side. You were in the van."

Gruff smiled at him and gathered Lyle into his arms, careful of his sprained wrist. "I jumped at the last second. My brothers pulled me up."

Lyle scowled at him. "Why the hell didn't you jump with me?"

"I didn't think about it," Gruff admitted. "I just wanted to make you were safe."

Lyle sat up. "You idiot, Gruff. You could have died. I saw you go over the side. Do you know what that did to me?"

Uh-ho. Now Lyle was calling him Gruff. He really was unhappy. Gruff held Lyle as tenderly as he could.

"I didn't mean to upset you, my darling boy. All I could think of that you were safe. You had to be safe."

Lyle curled the fingers of his right hand around Gruff's jacket. "My life means nothing. It's only you that's important."

"Could you two be more sappy?" PJ grumbled.

"Fuck off," Gruff muttered.

"A dollar," the three brothers chorused.

Gruff glowered at them. "I nearly died. Give me a break."

"Uh-huh." Alec shook his head. "There is precedence, remember? Brad and the woodchipper. That incident cost him twenty-eight dollars."

Lyle stared. "Should I ask?"

"Brad's jacket got caught, and if it hadn't been for Harry, we might be down to six brothers. Brad swore for a good ten minutes afterward. Mom still made him put the money in the jar."

Gruff had been a kid at the time but he remembered how shocked Brad had been and the way none of them left him alone all evening. He didn't remember Brad cursing for twenty-eight dollars' worth, but he knew Alec would be right. His brother was like that.

PJ looked up at the sound of sirens and grimaced. "This isn't going to be easy to explain to the sheriff."

"Where's Damien?" Lyle asked, as he and Gruff got to their feet.

He got the answer to that three minutes later when the sheriff's vehicle pulled up and a deputy stepped out to open the back door. Damien, Harry, and Brad almost tumbled over each other in their haste to get to Gruff and Lyle.

Damien reached them first and Gruff just had time to take in the large lump on his forehead before he found himself enfolded in Damien's arms and to his shock, he realized Damien was shaking.

"I couldn't bear it if it happened again."

Damien sobbed and Gruff held him close.

"It's okay," he soothed, finding himself being the one to comfort his older brother.

He knew Damien was talking about their parents. He had been the one to find them.

"I couldn't lose you. Or Lyle. I couldn't lose either of you."

As Gruff held his brother, he caught Lyle's shocked and pleased expression. Damien had included him in the family.

Then all the brothers crowded around them. He held out his hand and drew Lyle in, but no one said a word to Damien, just patting him on the back until Damien had gotten over his emotional storm.

"Give me your phone," Harry ordered.

Gruff unlocked it and handed it over.

"Don't you ever put it on silent again." Harry fiddled with it and returned it to Gruff.

"Who is going to tell me what happened?" the sheriff asked sourly.

Damien wiped his eyes and raised his head to look at Sheriff DeSantis, who was almost as tall as Gruff but built like a reed.

"David Rogerson kidnapped Lyle Parker and then tried to kill him and my brother."

DeSantis curled his lip. "So you say. Where is Mr. Rogerson?"

Gruff pointed at the edge. "Down there."

"And how did he end up down there?"

Lyle stepped forward and Gruff moved next to him. "You may not believe them, but you have to believe me. I was traveling with Damien into town. The CEO—" He noticed the sheriff's eyes go wide at the mention of his title, but he didn't stop to find out what that meant. "—forced our truck off the road by cutting the brakes."

Damien pointed at the lump on his head.

Lyle continued. "Then he kidnapped me with Mr. Hunter's help and forced me into the van. He was taking me back to Kingdom Mountain."

"Taking you back?" DeSantis queried.

"I was one of the orphanage boys."

Gruff laid a hand on Lyle's shoulder to give him comfort.

The sheriff's eyes narrowed, but he said, "Go on."

"I reached eighteen this week. They drugged me and left me in the forest to die."

"You can't say that," DeSantis protested.

"Yes, I can. When I didn't die, the CEO tried to pretend I was married to him, but Gruff realized that was a lie. Then he tried to poison me but poisoned Gruff instead. Then he kidnapped me."

"You know I'm telling the truth," Lyle insisted.

"And how do I know that?" The sheriff eyed him with dislike.

"Because you didn't get a call to come find my body. Something went wrong and Rogerson tried to fix it. Only he failed."

"It's a fancy tale, Mr. Parker," DeSantis said. "But it looks to me as if you murdered the CEO of Kingdom Mountain."

It was all bluster, and Gruff knew it. From the sick expressions on the faces of the deputies standing nearby, they knew it too. The sheriff's world had just imploded. He just didn't know it yet. Gruff didn't care.

Gruff wrapped Lyle in his arms and held him close, loving the way his boy burrowed in close to him. "You can say that but there's one thing you're forgetting."

"What's that?"

"We can prove every word."

Chapter 12

LYLE

Lyle felt sick just walking through the empty theme park. Now he hung onto Gruff's hand as tight as he could with his uninjured right hand. The paramedics had taken care of their injuries. Both he and Gruff had come out of it lightly considering. Even his wrist wasn't too bad once it had been bandaged and supported.

The adrenaline that had kept him going since the moment he woke up to see Rogerson sneering at home was fading fast. Lyle wanted to go home and curl up in Gruff's arms. His new home with Gruff. The theme park would never be his home again. The villain was dead, Gruff had kissed him and woken him up, the story was over, surely. Except this was real life and it didn't stop at 'they lived happily ever after.'

It was eerie being in the empty park. There was always someone around, even if it was the younger boys collecting the trash. But now he had no idea where anyone was, although he knew the cops had shut the place down to the public. Deputy sheriffs acted as their escort as they walked past the silent rides. He wasn't sure if the cops were guarding them or protecting them. The sheriff had listened to their story while they sat at on the mountain road and asked the same questions over and over. But their story hadn't budged, and eventually the sheriff had told them to wait in the theme park.

"I've got you, boy." Gruff bent to whisper in his ear. "You're mine. I'll never let you out of my sight."

Lyle looked up at him. "You promise?"

"I promise," Gruff said solemnly, stopping to seal the promise with a kiss.

"Put him down," Harry grumbled, somewhere behind them.

Lyle and Gruff ignored him. They needed the moment of intimacy to reconnect. Lyle didn't think he'd ever forget the split-second glimpse of watching Gruff go over the edge of the road. It had knocked the consciousness from Lyle like a blow to the head.

"Lyle! Lyle!"

The sound of his name distracted him. He turned to see a teenage boy running toward him.

"Vinny."

He stepped away from Gruff and braced himself, holding his left arm away from him to protect it. As he expected the boy slammed into him, not even stopping as he talked a mile a minute. Vinny was short and skinny, but he packed a punch, and Lyle staggered back even being prepared. Cops tried to grab hold of the boy, but Alec and Jake got between them. Lyle focused his attention on Vinny, but he knew Gruff was behind him.

"They said the CEO is dead. And you disappeared. And now you're back. And Hunter's gone. Where is he? The cops told us to wait in the dorm. But I saw you. And I knew it was you. You came back to rescue us, didn't you?"

Lyle waited until Vinny ran out of breath and stopped babbling. Then he smiled down at him. "Are you all right?"

The smile slipped off the boy's face. "When you didn't come back from the kitchen, we knew what had happened."

Lyle nodded. "I woke up in the forest down there. I was lucky. Someone found me."

"You were lucky." Vinny shivered. "The green coats said you'd found a job."

"You know that's a lie."

All the boys knew what happened once they reached eighteen.

Gruff put his arm around Lyle's shoulders and Lyle leaned into him, needing his support. "Vinny, it it? My name's Gruff."

Vinny's expression was wary, but he didn't take his eyes away from the way Gruff held Lyle. "That's a funny name."

"I know, it's really Greg, but they keep calling me Gruff." Gruff pointed at his brothers then turned back to Vinny. "Vinny, how did you escape from...uh...the green coats?"

Vinny licked his lips, clearly nervous. He glanced at the deputies and then back at Gruff

"It's okay, Vinny, you can tell me," Gruff assured him.

"I hid when they were rounding up the boys."

"That's very clever of you," Gruff's praise seemed to relax the boy until his next question. "Where are the green coats now?"

"I don't know."

Lyle became aware of the deputy sheriffs listening intently to their conversation. He fixed his gaze on the boy. "Vinny, you've got to tell the truth. Where are the green coats?"

Vinny wrung his hands. "I can't tell you. You're not one of us anymore."

That hurt more than he expected. But Lyle knew he was only saying what he'd been told to say in the past. "Do they have the boys?"

A tiny nod.

Lyle looked at Gruff and then at the deputies. From their grim expressions they'd caught the nod too. He stepped closer to Vinny and took his hands. "Are they in the tower?"

The hitch of breath was enough.

"The tower?" Gruff asked.

"It looks like a magic castle, but it's not. It's not." Lyle shivered. Bad things happened there. Things he hadn't shared even with Gruff.

Vinny's face had taken the gray pallor of the sky. "The green coats said if we spoke to you, we'd disappear. Please don't make me disappear. Please don't, Lyle."

Vinny was almost eighteen. The threat was real. Before Lyle could speak, Damien appeared at Lyle's side and Vinny shrank back in fear.

Lyle smiled up at Damien, laying a hand on his large forearm, and then at Vinny. "Vinny, this is Damien. He's Gruff's oldest brother. He looked big and scary, but he's not really."

Damien looked at the terrified boy. "Vinny, did the green coat actually say you'd disappear? Did he use those words?"

Vinny nodded. "They say that as a threat all the time."

"We've got them," one of deputies said with grim satisfaction. "Now we know what they were doing to the kids."

Lyle held back his angry words. The sheriff already knew. He was a friend of the evil man. But his fury must have been plain because the deputy narrowed his eyes.

"We've got to get the boys first," Damien said before either of them spoke. "Vinny, I promise you won't disappear. I will take care of you."

Vinny stared up at him. "You're real big. Are you sure you're not a green coat?"

Damien knelt in front of him. "I'm not a green coat. I promise."

"He's kinda grumpy, but he's one of the good guys," Gruff promised and Lyle nodded.

"Gruff has a lot of brothers. They took care of me."

"I'm scared," Vinny admitted. "I think the green coats have a plan to escape. I heard them talking about a tunnel from the magic castle."

Gruff furrowed his brow. "Are they going to take the boys somewhere else? They must know the game is up."

"They'll leave the boys behind and start again somewhere else," Lyle suggested.

"We've got to get to the tunnel before they

make their escape," the deputy said. "If only we knew where it came out."

To Lyle's surprise, PJ gave a wicked grin.

"I bet I know where that tunnel emerges. Remember, Brad? When we were kids? We found that tunnel up the top?"

Brad snapped his fingers. "I remember. It was locked at that end."

"We've got to head them off before they get out of there," the oldest deputy said.

"It's a long tunnel," PJ assured them. "And it comes out at the top of our land. They've got a long walk if they plan to go that way."

Damien was back on his feet and holding Vinny's hand. Lyle held back a smile. Neither Damien or Vinny seemed to notice.

"Are we free to go? We can get back to our land and get to the tunnel," Damien asked.

"All except you and you." One of the cops pointed at Gruff and Lyle. "You've still got questions to answer. Three of us will go with you. I'll call for backup too."

Vinny tugged at Damien's hand. "Don't leave me. You promised to take care of me."

Damien looked down at him. He seemed torn, but he'd made a promise. "It's okay, Vinny. I'll stay here with here with you." He looked up to see his six brothers staring at him open-mouthed. "What?" he snarled.

"We've got to find the boys in case..." Lyle trailed off, not daring to voice his fears.

"In case what?" Vinny asked suspiciously.

Gruff held Lyle closer. "We'll find them, I

promise. This is our fairy tale."

GRUFF

Gruff held his boy in his arms as his brothers and the cops conferred before they headed back in the direction of their farm. Damien was talking intently to Vinny. From the way Vinny looked up into his eyes, no one else in the world existed but the two of them.

Despite his brave words to Lyle, Gruff wasn't sure they'd find the other boys alive. The green coats knew the boys had information that could identify them. They may not have their names, but they had descriptions.

Lyle tilted his chin to look up at him. "What's wrong, Daddy? You feel so tense."

"I'll feel better when we find the boys," Gruff admitted.

"Do you think the green coats will hurt them?"

"What do you think? You know them better than anyone." As Lyle bit his lip Gruff frowned. There was something his boy wasn't telling him. "Lyle?"

"The green coats used to be boys. All of them. The CEO kept ten at a time to serve him. They were usually the bullies, but they did everything he asked. When...if...they rebelled, he disappeared them too."

"So they were under his control as well?"

Lyle nodded, his expression grim. "They were horrible to us. We all hated them. But becoming a green coat was one of the few ways to survive past eighteen. I was never going to be a green coat."

"No, you weren't," Gruff agreed. "You are loving and kind. There's no way you'd ever be horrible and mean to anyone. We need to get to the castle."

"I don't want to go back there," Vinny shrieked and threw himself into Damien's arms.

Damien gave Vinny a peculiarly tender look and then glanced over his head at Gruff, who smirked at him. He scowled and Gruff smirked even harder.

Lyle seemed to miss the byplay because he said, "You stay here with Damien, Vinny. We'll find them."

Vinny sobbed and held onto Damien.

They headed to the magic castle. It was the first time Gruff had seen the actual building that adorned the products from Kingdom Mountain. Gruff looked up at the fairy tale building in awe.

"It's so beautiful," he murmured.

"It's fake beauty," Lyle said, and Gruff turned to look at him at his harsh tone. "It's full of pain and hurt. Rogerson and the green coats lived here. You see beauty, I see evil."

Gruff enfolded Lyle in his arms. "You'll never have to see that again," he promised.

"Mr. Parker," one of the deputies said. "Where do you think the boys are?"

"In the tower." Lyle pointed up at the tallest tower with a delicate spire.

"We're going in," the deputy said. "You stay here."

Gruff knew Lyle wanted to argue, so he nodded, saying, "We'll wait here." He wasn't going to put his boy in danger.

The deputies disappeared inside the huge wooden doors of the castle. Gruff held Lyle and crooned to him, so he couldn't focus on anything except him.

They waited for what felt like fifteen agonizing minutes, then the doors opened, and a stream of boys flooded out, of varying ages, all dressed in the same shabby uniform of green and black. They shrieked when they saw Lyle and ran to them. Lyle freed himself from Gruff, and suddenly he was surrounded and Gruff found himself pushed further away as Lyle hugged each boy.

"They locked them in the tower."

Gruff turned to see the grim-faced deputy standing next to him. "What?"

"The green coats. They locked all the children in the tower and told them they would be beaten if they made a sound."

Bastards!

"Where are they? The green coats?" Gruff choked out. "Where are they?"

"The kids think they went through the tunnel." The deputy swallowed. "That room. It was vile. I..." He walked away, unable to speak.

Gruff looked over at his boy, now on his knees, talking to two boys of about five, both with tears streaming down their dirty faces.

Gruff's phone rang. It was Alec. He beckoned Lyle over, who disentangled himself from one of the small boys with some difficulty, handing him over to a tall, stocky boy who was at least half a foot taller than Lyle.

Gruff connected the call and put it on speaker. "Say that again, Alec."

"We've got them." Alec's voice boomed out of the speaker. "All the green coats. Ten of them. They're in police custody now."

Lyle stared at the phone as if he couldn't quite believe what he was hearing. "You've got them all?"

"We have. And get this. They're ready to talk. In fact, we can't shut them up. And the sheriff, he's not going to be happy."

Gruff frowned. "What do you mean?"

"Let's just say he's up to his eyeballs in shit. He's in custody too. Yeah, yeah, I'll pay the dollar," Alec snapped at someone.

Gruff glanced at Lyle and Vinny. Neither of them looked surprised. Lyle had said the sheriff was involved. It seemed he was right.

"Thanks, Alec. Is everyone all right?"

"We're fine, although PJ nearly fell down a shaft. Yes, you did, don't lie. Did you find the boys?"

Gruff grinned as he heard PJ's protests. "We did."

"What's going to happen to them?" Alec asked.

"There's a hundred boys to find homes for. At the moment, we've got no idea." Gruff disconnected the call and beckoned Lyle over to him.

Lyle curled his fingers in Gruff's jacket. "I can't leave them, Daddy. They need me."

"I know, my boy. I know."

Gruff kissed Lyle to reassure him, but maybe trying to reassure himself that he wouldn't lose his boy to the impossible task of finding homes for a hundred orphaned kids.

His work over for the morning, Gruff returned home in need of coffee and his boy. The kitchen was empty aside from Vinny, who was peeling a large mound of potatoes with a scowl on his face. Vinny was the newest resident of the cabin.

"Hi, Vinny. Where's Lyle?"

"Upstairs. He's pretending to change the beds. He left me to peel potatoes."

Vinny sounded so disgusted Gruff laughed.

"He made me peel the potatoes too."

"I thought I'd gotten out of the kitchen." Vinny sighed as if his world had come to an end.

"Did he spend all morning with the boys?"

"Of course." Vinny shrugged as if that were a given.

Gruff gritted his teeth. He was going to have to talk to his boy about managing his time. Lyle spent hours traveling to visit each boy from the orphanage. Many of them were struggling badly in their new foster homes and seeing a familiar face eased their fears. Lyle wanted to bring them back under one roof. Child Protective Services were adamant that was the wrong thing to do. Gruff erred on agreeing with the authorities, but after being abandoned by them, he knew Lyle would never agree to anything they said. He just hoped time and a lot of therapy would help the kids. Meanwhile Alec and Jake were trying to trace any relatives of the children.

"Have you seen Damien?" Vinny asked.

Gruff found the burgeoning relationship between Damien and Vinny bizarre. Damien treated Vinny like he was an adopted son and Vinny was determined to get Damien into bed. His brothers had their money on Vinny, but Gruff was sure Damien wouldn't consider touching him until he was eighteen.

"He'll be in soon."

Gruff backed out of the kitchen and took the stairs two at a time. He snuck into their bedroom, grinning at the sight of Lyle curled up in a ball, sleeping peacefully on the unmade bed. He tip-toed over to the bed, bent down and kissed him on the lips.

Lyle opened his eyes and smiled. "Daddy."

Gruff stroked his hair. "My boy, you look so good."

"What are you doing here?" Lyle yawned and stretched.

"Coming to find my little sleepy boy." Gruff tickled him and Lyle writhed and giggled.

"Do you want to sleep with me?"

Gruff shook his head. "No, I want you to come with me." It was time he gave his boy some devoted Daddy/boy time.

Lyle struggled to sit up. "I'm awake now. What do you want me to do?"

Gruff held out his hand and pulled his boy to his feet. Lyle curled into Gruff's arms.

"Where are we going?"

"Into the little bedroom."

"Vinny's room?"

"He's moved into the room next to Damien's."

It had been a storage room until that morning. But Vinny said he had nightmares and only Damien could soothe them. And what Vinny wanted, he got. Damien didn't notice any of the smirks from his brothers.

Gruff led him down the hall and into the bedroom at the end. Lyle stared at the change in the room.

"What's happened to the bed?"

In the place of the small bed was a large red winged armchair, a small table, and a bookcase.

"Now in Vinny's new room."

Gruff tugged Lyle over to the chair, sat down, and pulled Lyle down on top of him. He settled his lover until they were both comfortable in the chair.

Lyle snuggled into his, inhaling his scent as if it gave him comfort. "This is nice. But why are we in here?"

Gruff leaned around him and picked up a book. It was a children's book with colorful pictures.

Lyle frowned at the book. He recognized the story even if he couldn't read the words. "Are you going to read a kid's book to me?"

"I think it's time you learned to read and write," Gruff said.

Lyle traced the words of the title with one fingertip as if he were trying to memorize them. "Are you sure?"

Gruff kissed the top of his head. "I'm sure, my

boy. I thought we'd start with *Snow White*."

The End

A note from Sue Brown

I didn't know which brother I'd write next, but Vinny turned out to be very loud in my head, and what Vinny wants, Vinny gets.

Beau Bear, is a hurt/comfort, happy ever after romance based on a retelling of the *Ugly Duckling*.

Snow Twink was originally part of the M/M Fairy Tale Romance Series, a one-off story that spawned a whole series. Seven Daddy Bears had to have their own series, didn't they? *Bearytales in the Wood* was spawned. I always wanted to write a gay version of Seven Brides for Seven Husbands type story and a heartwarming, hurt/comfort Seven Boys for Seven Daddies was even better!

Here's a teaser from Beau Bear
Damien age 12

Damien rushed into the cabin, smiling as he heard his mother cooing at her new-born. All his chores done, it was his turn to cuddle his baby brother. The rest of his brothers laughed at him, but they all knew the oldest of the Brenner boys loved them fiercely and protectively, and the latest addition to the Brenner household was no exception. At school, they'd told him that baby birds followed their mother because she was the first face they saw. He couldn't be the first face of course, because his mom and dad were their parents, but he firmly believed in imprinting on his baby brothers as soon as possible. It seemed to work too. They followed him all the time.

Damien loved his six brothers, but as the oldest, a lot of the responsibility for looking after the older boys fell on him, while his mom took care of the little ones. With his dad working on their Christmas tree farm all the time, he was more like a father-figure to them. He hoped, maybe, his mom and dad would stop asking the stork to bring them a girl. It was obvious the bird was a boy stork who only brought boys.

But then he heard another woman speak and grimaced. It was their neighbor. New babies always brought lots of people to the cabin. Damien couldn't understand why. By the seventh boy he'd have thought the novelty would have worn off, but they still flocked to the cabin.

"Oh Mollie, the little one is gorgeous. What are you going to call him?"

In Damien's opinion, some visitors were more welcome than others. He didn't like old Mrs. Viner. She was always trying to interfere in the way his mom did everything from bringing up the kids to cooking the dinner. His dad said it was because her husband and son ignored her. Her son had just taken a job in the Kingdom Mountain Theme Park just up the mountain. Mrs. Viner was very proud of him. He got to wear a green coat, and she showed everyone a photo of him in his uniform. But she was always complaining he never visited her, and he was only just up the mountain road.

"His name is Gregory, but Jake calls him Gruff."
His mom sounded weary. "They all call him Gruff
now."

"Little Gruff," Mrs. Viner chuckled. "What's he?
Number seven?"

Damien's mom sighed. "Yes, but that's all now.
I've told Jimmy I've had enough. I'm just thankful
I have Damien to help me."

Damien wrinkled his nose at Mrs. Viner's
derisive hum. She was nasty, but no matter how
often he told his mom, she just told him not to be
rude. He had to respect Mrs. Viner.

"Well, your Damien has to be good for
something. He's never going to be a looker. Your
boys certainly improved the more you had. This
one is as cute as a button."

Damien waited for his mom to defend him, to
say he was beautiful or something. But all she said
was "He's a young and growing lad. He's got time
to improve."

Mrs. Viner sniffed. "He's certainly an ugly
duckling compared to this little man. He won't be
handsome enough to become a green coat like *my*
Eddie."

"We need Damien to work on the farm," his
mom said mildly. "The theme park can do
without his help."

Damien flinched as they discussed his future
like he had no say in the matter. He'd always
wanted to get off the mountain and travel the
world. He had a huge picture of the world pinned
up in his bedroom, and he entertained his little

brothers by getting them to pick a place on the map and telling them all about the country.

"Let's hope he finds a girl who doesn't care that he's not a looker," Mrs. Viner said.

"Looks aren't everything. Damien's got a kind heart," Damien's mom protested.

Damien rocked back on his heels. He was consumed with hatred for Mrs. Viner, but the biggest betrayal was his mom. Damien was crushed by his mom's lack of support. She thought he was ugly. He bit his lip against the sudden tears in his eyes. He wouldn't cry. He was a big boy now. Crying was for little kids. He wiped at his eyes impatiently. It didn't matter that he wasn't handsome. He was never going to get married, and he didn't like girls anyway. They had cooties.

He backed away from the kitchen, needing to find somewhere to hide. He needed time to get over the hurt in his heart at his mother's betrayal. He'd hide at the woodshed. No one would follow him there.

Before he could run away, a cry went up from the main room.

"Damie, I lost my Legos." PJ ran toward him, his face smeared with dirt and tears. "They were here and now they're gone."

Damien opened his mouth to yell that he didn't care about Legos, but then he saw PJ's expression and his heart melted as it always did where his brothers were concerned.

"We put them away last night, remember? So Mom wouldn't trip over them and drop little

Gruff."

"But my spaceship was going to Mars," PJ wailed.

Damien *oofed,* staggering back as PJ ran into him. At six years old, PJ was already tall and broad enough to leave bruises.

"Easy, buddy." At least Damien could explain away the tears now. "Your spaceship is in one piece. Let's take the Legos box upstairs and you can play with them in my bedroom."

PJ nodded, all smiles now. "You can play with me, but not Jakey, cos he breaks things."

Jake was two. He broke a lot of things. Damien spent a lot of time stopping the older brothers from yelling at Jake.

"Let's sneak up," Damien suggested.

PJ grinned and tip-toed to the stairs.

Damien retrieved the Legos box from the playroom and followed PJ up the stairs. He caught sight of himself in the big mirror at the top of the stairs. Dark, floppy hair, square jaw, brown eyes. He looked like a younger version of his father. Damien frowned. His mom loved his dad despite that. Damien took a deep breath. It didn't matter what he looked like. He still didn't like girls.

What's happens to Damien when he grows up? Will the ugly duckling become a swan? Find out in the second Bearytales, ***Beau Bear.***

Also by Sue Brown

STANDALONE books

Summer's Dawn | Summer's Song | A Tale Told in Darkness | A Cock in the Window | In-Decision | The Backpack | The Clumsy Santa | Mr Plum | Chance to Be King | Made for Aaron | Final Admission | The Layered Mask | The Next Call | The Night Porter | Light of Day | The Sky Is Dead | Nothing Ever Happens | Stolen Dreams | Waiting | Prey Time | Louis Hates Valentines Day | Racing Raindrops | The Fireman's Pole Falling for Ramos | Last Place at the Chalet | Still Loving You

JT'S BAR series

His Shield | His Guardian | His Warrior | His Valentine | His Protector | His Sentinel | His Defender

BIKER DADDY BODYGUARDS

Hold Firm | Hold Close | Hold Safe | Hold Tight | Biker Daddy Bodyguards Boxset

DARKER DADDY BODYGUARDS

Dark Heart | Dark Secret | Dark Haven | Dark Angel

BEARYTALES IN THE WOOD

Snow Twink | Beau Bear | Boy Tangled | Jack's Giant | Boy Riding | Beauty & the Bear | Bear in Boots

ANGEL SECURITIES series

Morning My Angel | Goodnight My Angel | Hello My Angel | Angel Securities Boxset

LYON ROAD VETS series

Hairy Harry's Car Seat | Bob, the Destroyer of Leads | Hazel Takes Over | Stormin' Norman | Lyon Road Vets Boxset

DATING MR, RIGHT series

Speed Dating the Boss | Secretly Dating the Lionman | Slow Dating the Detective Dating Mr. Right Boxset

WITH A KICK series (with Clare London)

Hissed as a Newt | Bells and Balls

FRANKIE'S series

Frankie & Al | Ed & Marchant | Anthony & Leo |
Jordan & Rhys |

THE ISLE series
The Isle of... Where? | Isle of Wishes | Isle of
Waves | Isle of Waiting Island Doctor | Island
Counselor |Island Detective | Isle Series Boxset

SKANDIK & OWENS series
A Body in his Bed

MORNING REPORT series
Morning Report | Complete Faith | Go-to Guy |
Luke's Present | Letters From a Cowboy | Morning
Report Boxset

MULTI-AUTHOR
A Little Christmas! Danny
My Christmas Nemesis in Kind Hearts at
Christmas
Trickle of Blood in Gothika: Fang
A Boy Unleashed

About Sue Brown

Sue Brown is a Londoner with a dream to live on a small island. Coffee fuels her addiction for writing romance with hot guys loving each other, and her Adorkadog snores in harmony as she creates.

Come over and talk to Sue at:
Newsletter: http://bit.ly/SueBrownNews
Bookbub: https://www.bookbub.com/profile/sue-brown
Website: http://www.suebrownstories.com/
Facebook group:
https://www.facebook.com/SueBrownsStories/
Tiktok: https://www.tiktok.com/@suebrownstories
Email: sue@suebrownstories.com

Printed in Great Britain
by Amazon

43267448R00098